Molecular Ramjet

and other bedtime stories ...

by Larry G. Carlson, M.S.

TadAleX
Seattle, Washington

i

Published by:

TadAleX

P.O. Box Number 78582

Seattle, Washington 98178

Copyright © 1988 by Larry G. Carlson
First Printing 1989

Library of Congress Catalog Card Number: 88-51121

ISBN 0-929301-01-3 Softcover

These stories are works of fiction. The **SETI** project and **The Planetary Society** are real (*see Glossary*). However, the U.L.I.A.R. project and all names, characters, and incidents are products of the author's imagination. Any resemblance to actual events or persons, living or dead, is entirely coincidental.

I thank God for my loving, supportive wife, LaDonna, without whom this book would never have been possible, and for our children, Alex, Tad, and Rachael ... who love to hear bedtime stories

Upcoming books by the author

Red, Blue, Yellow, Green

- *Red, Blue, Yellow, Green*

- *Quaternary Dispersion*

- *Robert's Window*

Nanoinvasion

- *Nanoinvasion*

- *Ambassador for Life*

- *The Snake*

FOREWORD

Reading and storytelling can prepare a young child for later school years and continue to support older children as well. Recognition of the necessity of reading and storytelling with our pre-schoolers has never been more publicized than today. Yet many parents feel their duties in this area, and yes, their joys as well, end with the children's entrance into school. And after all, once the young people have been exposed to the carefully planned lessons at school, and are old enough to fully appreciate the really 'good' programs available on television, what can we offer? Among other things, we can offer the same exciting, loving storytelling and reading that kept them in rapt attention for the first five years of their lives.

Particularly since the advent of the nuclear age, science fiction has become widely popular. Yet, this category of fiction often lacks acceptance among much of literary society - too often for good reason. A substantial portion of available science fiction utilizes unwarranted violence, sex, and profane language as selling ploys. Just as prevalent, but more insidious are stories which are subtley or overtly demeaning of the human condition and antithetic of an immortal spirit. These characteristics are not restricted exclusively to science fiction writings. On the contrary, science fiction, can be an ideal medium to spark the young mind to hunger, to read and to wonder. Well written science fiction can:

- *Prepare young minds to ask important questions.*

- *Aid young readers in accepting the radical changes occurring in the world around them.*

- *Generate an interest in scientific endeavors.*

- *Develop an awareness of some of the dogmas and dilemmas facing the technologically advancing society.*

- *Help students become familiar with today's scientific terminology so they will not feel threatened by terms like deoxyribonucleic acid (DNA), genetic engineering, plasma, nucleus and inclusion bodies when they enter science classes.*

- *Prompt young readers to create stories of their own.*

Reading should not always be a solitary endeavor. Correct grammar is learned first and foremost in the hearing. Although many young people have not yet been exposed to formal grammatic terms and rules for properly spoken english, they can be taught to appreciate correct english 'by ear'. All of the '**... and Other Bedtime Stories**' collections are purposely written using a somewhat advanced vocabulary range to tell fast moving, exciting science fiction stories. Parents may wish to read the stories alone first and take advantage of the glossary of terms at the end of the books.

When will your children outgrow good bedtime stories? Well, let's see ... I'm over 40 ...

Larry

MOLECULAR

RAMJET

CHAPTER 1

The basement shop turned laboratory was a mess. Charles and Beth Willow allowed their special children considerable freedom in selecting their hobbies as long as they continued to maintain exemplary grades and proceeded in a safety-conscious manner. The first condition had always been met; the second tended to slip once in a while. Both parents were professors at the university and had done considerable 'tinkering' themselves when they were young, and so were particularly sensitive to their children's needs in this area.

Their eldest, Jim, was presently in a rocket engine phase. Jim, a natural leader and a certifiably brilliant concrete, sequential thinker, had always been a dreamer too. His specialty was to design a research project and painstakingly follow through with all phases of the enterprise.

Bob, the second sibling of the Willow clan, had an uncanny ability to join seemingly unrelated facts into unique theories, jumping over the drudgery of carefully planned research. This facet of his personality did not always endear him to his meticulous older brother. Bob was into lasers.

Last to bless Charles and Beth was Tina, nick-named Little-T by her brothers. She was not the stereotypical little sister. Little-T, a born engineer, was more likely to be found at a table saw or lathe than with dolls. The young lady had developed the tough, confident personality that was necessary for her to survive amidst the two older brothers. Right now she was finishing cutting the main core to Jim's latest attempt at a model ramjet engine.

Bob turned on a bathtub-design, gas-powered laser. A small pencil of light jumped between multiple mirrored surfaces balanced on small stands to impinge on a photoelectric meter. Bob twiddled knurled knobs on the side of his apparatus. At the same time a small splinter of hot metal flew off Little-T's cutting tool and settled on her exposed wrist. Reflex jerked her arm back uncontrollably. The cutting tool in her hand knocked over one of the teetering laser mirrors. The runaway beam passed through several glass prisms dangling from part of a scavenged chandelier creating a spectacular, but unexpected, light show. One of the stray rays of light centered on Jim's left cornea blinding him momentarily. Jim jumped up from his work bench, banging his head on a low overhead timber.

Without even thinking to ask if Little-T had been hurt, both boys yelled at her, "Hey, watch what you're doing Tee!"

Little-T glared at her brothers for their lack of sensitivity and removed the tapered hollow tube from the lathe. Throwing it to Jim, the metal still warm from the last cutting, she said, " It's done anyway."

The three youngsters had not yet learned to work well as a team. That would change.

Jim reassembled the ramjet using Little-T's new part. Once everything seemed in order, he filled a small black rubber bladder with fuel. He connected a dry cell battery to two terminals located on the top of the main thruster and blew warm air down the throat of his engine with the remnants of an old portable hair dryer. Without even a cough to warn the other occupants of the room, the ramjet ignited with a remarkably loud sustained roar. It hadn't occurred to Jim to mention to his brother and sister that he was going to ignite the jet.

Little-T and Bob nearly died of fright. Charles was reading the paper upstairs. The open newspaper jerked spasmodically for an instant before Jim's dad regained control. He looked over at his wide-eyed wife simultaneously rolling his eyes toward the ceiling and shrugging his shoulders, then returned to his paper. Charles and Beth were use to unusual noises from the basement.

Having recovered from the shock, Jim's siblings came over to watch the model engine. When the noise died, Bob and

Little-T both pounded Jim on the back. "Awesome, truly radical," they agreed. The children always reveled in each others accomplishments despite the occasional bickering. Previous squabbles were instantly forgotten in the admiration of success.

Returning to his laser, Bob picked up a large ring, superconducting magnet his father had scrounged from the remains of a previous university research project. Bob had been studying the possible effects the strong magnetic field might have on the excited gas ions used to generate his laser beam.

He paused, arms frozen in the mid air, and eyed Jim's ramjet engine. He wondered if the ramjet's plasma stream would be affected by the strong magnetic field the superconductor produced. "Say, Jim, let's see what effect a high density magnetic field would have on the plasma stream in your new ramjet engine," Bob offered.

Jim was not particularly enthusiastic about having Bob try one of his hare-brained schemes on his new toy, but his inquisitive nature got the best of him and he agreed to a test. Jim refilled the fuel bladder and prepared to start the model engine. Bob separated the superconducting ring into its two parts and placed it around the ramjet body. Plugging the magnet into the heavy transformer sitting on the floor, he told Jim to "Let her rip." Jim, standing at the front of the work bench, leaned over and started the ramjet with the hair drier once more. The small engine began immediately with another loud blast, however, this time the ear shattering buzz skyrocketed to a much higher frequency and a 30 foot long plasma display pierced the basement room. The unstable ion wash immediately blossomed into three sections that spread out like the petals of a giant flower. The heavy wooden work table on which Jim had fastened his project began to move. Jim and the table were carried toward the wall in back of him. At the last moment the table caught between two support pillars saving Jim's body from being crushed against the far wall. Upstairs, Charles dropped his paper and jumped up. A copper display plate hanging on the front room wall turned cherry red from an induced electric current, melted and collapsed to the floor. Beth ran from the kitchen where, Charles noticed, all the metal pans had rushed to one side of the room and were dancing on the far wall. The incredible racket stopped as suddenly as it had begun. The parents ran to the stairs leading to the basement and plunged down. The shop had been nearly demolished. Jim was backed against one wall of the shop, eyes open wider than Charles had thought possible. Slowly all five family members moved to examine the glowing ramjet engine.

CHAPTER 2

that summer ...

Charles and Beth agreed to assist their young inventors in the building of a larger prototype of the ramjet engine on the condition that they would not ignite the engine in their home. During the following months every spare dime and all recreational time went into the building of a new ramjet model. Bob determined that the magnetic field was, in fact, resulting in synchronous emission of the energized plasma ions not unlike the synchronous emission of light from a laser. He dubbed their project the 'Molecular RamJet' engine. Charles and Beth plagued their colleagues at the university with requests for information and excess laboratory gear. Slowly the family's efforts came to fruition and the new prototype took shape in the reconditioned basement laboratory. It was time to go to the farm.

Excitement was high during the trip across the mountains to the farm of Beth's parent. The rapid talking of the children blended together with the rumbling of the van's tires on the road until one was not distinguishable from the other. Upon arrival at the farm, the Willow family dispensed with the usual greetings. Rather than pull up the long driveway leading to the large two story farmhouse, Charles brought the car around to the edge of a grassy field. Grandpa Don and Grandma Loreta emerged from the farmhouse and looked suspiciously at the large metal sled being unloaded from the van into the neighboring field. It was a heavy metal contraption with substantial metal runners supporting a pallet of heavy batteries. Cradled above the batteries on thick iron legs was a 4 foot long cylinder, open at both ends. A 15 inch diameter superconducting magnet surrounded the ominous looking cylinder. The large ramjet prototype stood out in sharp contrast against a backdrop of velvet grasses and grazing cattle. Beth had warned her parents that the children were coming to the farm to test another one of their projects. Considering some of the previous experiences grandpa and grandma had faced at the hands of their precocious grandchildren, Don and Loreta's consent was a true witness of their love for their daughter and her family.

"What is that thing, some new kind of tractor?" grandpa teased.

"Not exactly," Jim responded. "Could you bring around the big John Deer tractor and hook the power drive for the corn grinder over here?" he requested pointing to the old mill at the edge of the field.

A pleading nod from his daughter sent Don to the barn. Soon the low, pounding sound of a diesel engine announced his return. Grandpa maneuvered the great tractor expertly into place just to the rear of the sled and close enough to the grinder so the power belt would be stretched taut.

"So this thing is a fancy corn mill?" grandpa guessed again. The children were now too busy getting their project ready for its first test to defend themselves against any more of grandpa's teasing. Jim brought the flexible tube that normally shot the ground corn feed into burlap bags around to the front of the jet engine so it could be aimed down the metal monster's throat. One last request was for a long extension cord from the barn. Bob explained that the engine would have to be jump started at first with both air pressure and electricity. After that, the batteries would take over. Little-T busied herself filling a 5 gallon rubber fuel bladder with alcohol that they had brought with them from the city. All was in readiness. Charles suggested everyone, except Jim and Bob move over to the farm house as the engine might produce "some" noise.

Jim started the tractor and, standing to one side, forced air from the corn mill through the sleeping ramjet. Bob, waiting for a nod from Jim, closed the circuit to the superconducting ring simultaneously opening a small fuel valve. Little-T picked up a video camera to document the first test firing of the new prototype. Just as Grandpa leaned over to ask Charles, above the throb of the tractor engine and power drive, if he thought the noise might be loud enough to bother the cows, an incredible sonic blast of hot air rocked the valley. A plasma display over 100 feet long screamed from the end of the terrible machine. The asphalt in the street behind the machine boiled and caught fire. Grandpa's great John Deer tractor was also caught in the blast. The beautiful green paint blackened and burned. The large tires melted. Farmhouse windows shattered. Within a fraction of a second the thrust from the molecular ramjet was too much and the engine tore loose from its mountings. It seemed to hesitate for a split second then accelerated across the field at a furious rate. Two unsuspecting cows that had been slowly grazing across Grandpa's field had the misfortune of being in the trajectory of the escaped ramjet engine. Two red billowing clouds blossoming down field signalled the bovines' passage into another life. The engine was now invisible to the eye, but its final destination became clear as there was an enormous blast in the Horse Heaven hills beyond the farm.

Silence followed. The corn grinder was laying on its side. The once beautiful tractor was a smoldering heap. Billows of dark black smoke rose from the burning tires. Jim and Bob, having jumped clear of the blast, were sitting in the field gawking at the destruction around them. Little-T stood open-mouthed, finger pulled tightly on the trigger of the video camera that was still hanging at her side. Grandma and Grandpa stared in disbelief at their tractor, then at Charles and Beth. "We may not be welcome on the farm again," thought Charles.

CHAPTER 3

later that year ...

Two things became immediately clear to Jim, Bob and Little-T's parents with the incident on the farm. First, their children were not normal, and second their research could no longer (and should no longer) be supervised by their parents alone. The next accident could do more harm than vaporize a few cows and several tons of hillside. To protect the children (children??) and the neighboring population, better administration and direction for their mental energies would have to be found. Over the children's din of some rational, but mostly irrational objections, that approached the decibel level of the first ramjet prototypes themselves, the parents formally contacted the University's Advanced Studies Foundation and asked for government intervention and financial support for the next stage of the molecular ramjet project. If the truth were known, the young researchers realized that they did not have the manufacturing facilities, the necessary funding, nor the organizational expertise to move from a basement prototype to a craft capable of carrying a human payload. They didn't, however, want the interference that was sure to come from government red tape.

To the Willow's surprise, formal appraisal of the primitive drawings and notes resulted in an immediate response by the Advanced Studies Office. Within only a few weeks (mere nanoseconds on the crawling bureaucratic clock) the young researchers had been asked to decide on a name for their team and to prepare for a move to a special school/research facility in New Mexico. There they would oversee the design and construction of a manned aircraft powered by a molecular ramjet engine. Remarkably, all three of the younger Willow's immediately agreed to the move far from home. Sadness at the prospect of leaving their friends and parents was mitigated by their intense interest in continuing their research - this time with funding only the government could supply.

Jim, Bob and Tee settled, after a considerable amount of debate and some prompting on the part of their parents, on 'Sibling Research Despite Sibling Rivalry' as an appropriate handle for their enterprise. Rather than the obvious acronym of SRDSR for a logo they selected the somewhat more obtuse, but intellectually satisfying $D(SR)^2$.

The relocation to the New Mexico facility went smoothly with the $D(SR)^2$ (dee-essarr-squared) team talking and planning considerably faster than the 65 mile-an-hour restriction on the transportation vehicles. After what seemed like weeks to the young researchers, but was actually only 3 days, the caravan arrived at the school/research facility in New Mexico. $D(SR)^2$'s new home was not at all what they expected. Here, literally in the middle of nowhere, was a small group of brick buildings baking in the desert sun. There had been no attempt to landscape the facility and the only thing larger than sage growing in the parched ground was a group of antennae and satellite dishes poised as if hopeful something would soon be descending from the skies. Vacationers or normal people would have refused to disembark, but this crew, seeing through the passion of attempting to relieve an urgent intellectual itch, bounded off the caravan and ran to the beautiful isolation of desolation that would allow uncompromised and uninterrupted scratching.

Before the day was out the barren camp was settled enough to allow the first board meeting between $D(SR)^2$ and the special government team representative, Steve. Steve's presentation was short and simple. He explained preliminary investigation of the $D(SR)^2$ molecular ramjet project had caused considerable excitement and it had been immediately decided to offer financial and expert assistance as required with only minimal contractual management. All research would proceed uninterrupted at whatever pace the team could manage. Equipment and supply requests would be handled by Steve without question. The only requirements made on the $D(SR)^2$ team would be that they would allow the government to maintain secrecy over the project until its completion and to select trained Air Force personnel to fly the first missions. Jim immediately bristled at the thought of letting someone else fly their dream machine, but decided being an expert test pilot was probably not in his repertoire of special gifts. The team conceded to the government requests.

It was further decided that the 'Molecular Ramjet' project would be divided into three main areas of interest: first, the development of a stable propulsion system capable of something other than the earth-wrenching, all-or-nothing blasts of the earlier prototypes; secondly, the design and construction of an aerodynamically stable craft to carry the propulsion unit and human cargo; and thirdly, the development of sophisticated communication and telemetry equipment. Jim was assigned leader of the propulsion laboratory. Tee was given supervision of the aircraft design division and Bob opted for communication instrumentation. The divisions were administrative only and although each researcher promised to spend most of their energies in their assigned divisions, it was also formally recognized that their minds could not be artificially trapped in one area. Daily meetings would allow input into any area of research by all members.

After a necessary, but not particularly interesting, late supper, the three young scientists fell onto military fashion cots. They tried to sleep while battling screaming cerebral currents that passed visions of riding never-before-seen aircraft, standing on a spectacular plasma stream, to the edge of space. They would never have slept at all if they had any hint of how conservative there wildest imaginings were and what was ahead for them ... and Earth itself.

CHAPTER 4

5 years later ....

Jim stared at the sleek black ship sitting on the launch pad in front of him. Behind him the small facility had grown into a town during production of the Manta. The original modest brick buildings were lost among new metal and steel construction. A long runway carved out of the desert floor stretched out away from Jim as far as the eye could see. Before him was the fruit of their efforts - an ominous black form of composite matrix outer skin that reflected almost no light giving it the appearance of a three dimensional shadow in the bright desert sun. The Manta, named after the marine life it closely resembled, was nearly ready for its maiden voyage.

The last 5 years had passed very quickly. As Jim waited for the last briefing of Air Force personnel before the first flight testing of Manta, his mind wandered. Since the project had begun, the $D(SR)^2$ team had only slept or eaten as an after-thought. Steve had more than lived up to his end of the bar-gain; giving not only financial support and materials to the project, but arranging expertise and training in every area of endeavor as needed. Manta would hold a crew of three: pilot, co-pilot, and navigations-communications officer. Work on the molecular ramjet propulsion unit itself had been rapid once it had been determined the strength of the magnetic field could be frequency pulsed without loosing molecular laser velocity. In addition, ejected mass would be reduced and controlled. Smooth, controlled acceleration was needed if the ship were to accommodate the weakly supported human frame.

The ship's outward design reflected the need for streamlining a craft that would approach Mach 5 within the Earth's atmosphere. Tee's windtunnel tests and computer modeling had revealed that no metal ship could withstand the temperatures and pressures of doing almost 4000 miles an hour within the Earth's atmosphere, so Manta had been made of special composites. The composites consisted mostly of graphite and titanium threads in a plastic and ceramic matrix. Even the materials for this ship had to be specially designed.

Bob had realized early on that heat build up around the ship and atmosphere ionization would preclude utilization of any conventional forms of communication. New forms of communications were developed. One utilized visible spectrum communication and the other mass movement gravitational waves (MMGVC). MMGVC was a radically new idea in communications theory and design. Bob had conceived the notion while listening to one of Jim's many long winded explanations of the advantages of frequency pulsed control of mass movement. If molecular motion within the bowels of the molecular ramjet engine could be controlled, Bob had reasoned the gravitational waves emanating from the artificially accelerated mass might be useful for communications as well. His intuitive understanding of the situation paid off big. A totally new form of communication - MMGVC - became one of many offshoots of the team's efforts. As often occurred in projects of this magnitude, resulting spin-off technologies were numerous. Hundreds of patents and new engineering and material science methodologies had been born from the construction of Manta. During the 5 year effort the members of the $D(SR)^2$ team had changed too. No longer children, but men and a full grown woman. There were no regrets. The molecular ramjet project had not stolen, but had been, their youth.

The ear piercing scream of audio feedback, which preceded all announcements from the facility PA system, jerked Jim back to normal space-time. Absently Jim noted the irony of using a 19th century PA systems at a facility building 21st century communications equipment. "Why hadn't Bob fixed that?" It was time for the $D(SR)^2$ team to have a last moment of preparation with the Air Force crew selected for Manta.

The three Air Force flight officers chosen were stereotypically perfect, down to using boyish nick-names at introduction time. The communications officer, Cornell, was a think-tanker from the university of the same name, high-spirited, but definitely mentally competent to understand the subtleties of MMGVC communication. The co-pilot, Ripper, was a blond, hot-shot fighter pilot whose main qualification for this team was having the fastest reaction times ever recorded in Air Force history. Tee's personal impression was that he had played one too many video games. Only the pilot, Hollywood, had been misnamed. He looked like anything but a hollywood star. Without sun glasses and flight suit, he was not impressive looking, nor did he outwardly radiate the high energy associated with fly boys. He gave the immediate impression of a man who would be completely stable in any situation. Like the astronauts who preceded him, Hollywood was not young and restless, but a hard experienced pilot who could be trusted with the 19 billion dollar Manta. The entire team agreed that Hollywood was the right man to command the first manned molecular ramjet mission. The young people found the last briefing dull and redundant, reviewing information and flight plans which had been reviewed many times before. Only Hollywood seemed totally consumed with knowing every jot and tittle of information. Like other surviving test pilots, he had every intention of returning the lives and equipment placed in his hands to the owners. The briefing was closed. As the crew and scientists walked the few hundred yards to the launch pad all conversation ceased. Even Ripper seemed to be caught up in anticipation of stepping into the unknown.

CHAPTER 5

first flight ...

With the crew on board and communications operational, the D(SR)^2 team listened to Hollywood's calm voice over the camp PA system as he chopped out orders and began the long pre-flight check list. After what seemed like forever to the young investigators standing outside, the final count down started. Hollywood's voice was calm as he began preflight. " 10, 9, 8, 7, 6, 5 ...engage frequency pulse generators ... 4, 3, 2, 1, 0."

At the count of 0 the air began to hum, not a high or loud hum at first, but a penetrating throb that was more felt than heard. Immediately the plasma display appeared from the rear of Manta. The hot gasses bent the light passing through them causing the desert floor on the opposite side of the ship began to shimmer and move. Quickly the hum changed to a scream. The ground crew threw on protective head gear as the decibel level passed the pain threshold. Just before Manta began to move the plasma jet changed to violet and the engine's scream reached an unbearable pitch. Sparks of static electricity danced in the air. Window panes in the closest buildings shattered. Manta hesitated momentarily, then accelerated down the runway. Cornell's voice reported acceleration in g forces counting from 1 to 4 as Manta began a nearly vertical climb to it's operational 100,000 feet. As they passed the 15,000 foot level, Hollywood ordered pressure suits and helmets sealed. At 100,000 feet, Ripper reported their position and speed,

Mach 2, to the scientists on the ground. Ripper knew the young scientists back on the desert floor were listening to every word and in a sense flying in the cockpit with him. He was careful to report as much information as possible without endangering the crew by neglecting his on-board duties. Tee would have been surprised at his sensitivity to their situation.

CHAPTER 6

elsewhere in space ...

Below, a glowing green-blue sphere hung in orbit. Beautiful to any eyes capable of visualizing electromagnetic radiation in the 4000 to 7000 angstrom range. Beyond were the stars, small but brilliant without the dulling effect of the Earth's atmosphere. Then a change occurred. Something went wrong with the fabric of space-time. A two dimensional line 50 miles long appeared, then opened into a circle. Unimaginable energies poured out from some other part of the galaxy as the circle became a sphere and even more dimensions were added. From the middle of this tangle of crossed dimensions floated a ship, roughly 30 miles in diameter. The hole in the universe closed leaving the ship quiet in space with only an outward blast of radiation to divulge that anything had occurred. The blast front raced toward earth at the speed of light.

CHAPTER 7

at 100,000 feet ...

With the emotionless tones of an experienced test pilot, Hollywood announced his intentions to attempt Mach 4.5. At 19 miles above the surface of the planet, there were no visual clues to indicate the speed they had already attained. Only a subtle change in the frequency of the earsplitting noise already emanating from the engine and the increased g forces would indicate further acceleration. At Hollywood's order, Ripper's hand moved to the set of bars that served as the ship's throttle and slowly began pushing them forward. Jim and the rest of the $D(SR)^2$ team could hear Ripper calling off velocity changes at intervals. Just as Ripper was calling out Mach 4.5, the Earth, was bathed in a blast of energy such as it had not felt since the solar system had begun to cool billions of years earlier. The skies lit up as if someone had just taken a flash photo of the earth with a mammoth camera. The $D(SR)^2$ team simultaneously intercepted static crackle from Manta communications. All three crew members spoke excitedly and at once. In the background, the frequency pulse failure alarm sounded. Both the Manta crew and the inventors on the desert floor knew exactly what this meant. Loss of pulsed frequency control to the engine during acceleration meant the molecular ramjet would run wild, full out, pumping acceleration past the limits the human body could withstand. Still in full control of himself, Hollywood requested Cornell report the ship's position before uncontrolled acceleration began. The ground support team saw the 25 mile plasma stream, indicating Manta had gone ballistic. A shrill scream followed seemingly crying out over the impending loss of life aboard. Hollywood's voice was strained now, not in fear, but under the pressure of a body that would soon weigh tons due to increasing g forces. The ship would out-live the crew, but eventually even the composite skin of Manta would give way as the artificial meteor melted from the heat of atmospheric friction.

Bob jumped to the microphone and yelled over the noise coming from the speaker transmissions from Manta. "Hollywood! Pull up ... pull up !!! Your only hope is to gain altitude!"

Just before passing out, Hollywood understood and obeyed Bob's command. He pulled up on the stick in an attempt to get above useful atmosphere. On the edge of space too few molecules of air would be available and they might be able to force Manta into a flame-out condition. Unfortunately, the velocity attained by the ship was too great and the last thing the crew saw before falling into the thick blackness of insufficient cerebral blood supply was Manta leaving the earth's gravitational field and streaking out into deep space. The noise of the alarms faded from the communication speakers in New Mexico as the last bit of air leaked out of the ship's cabin. Without air no sound traveled to the microphones that dangled in front of the unconscious crew. Ironically, Manta's trajectory would take the craft within visual range of only one object before leaving the solar system forever. That object was the new silver planetoid whose abrupt entrance into this part of space provoked the mishap that fused the ship's pulse frequency generator.

CHAPTER 8

U.L.I.A.R. complex ....

The personnel office at the U.L.I.A.R. complex was empty at 2 AM. The power indicator LED on a computer driven printer turned on. Quietly, a Class I request for an expert in computer generated intelligence was generated without human intervention. Another printer quickly produced a mailing envelope addressed to MIT. Form and envelope met at an automated sealer and the completed package fell into the outgoing mail chute. The additional letter would not be noticed by the day crew. The high priority personnel request was noted in the computer banks as having been initiated through regular channels. The power indicator light extinguished and the office slept again.

weeks later ...

Breeze - the phonetic translation of Barbara Reed Zandt's initials - had plenty of time to reflect on the occurrences of the last few days as she rode the small rail shuttle up the steep climb to over 9,000 feet. The drop in temperature told her that even during the summer the U.L.I.A.R. complex would be a chilly assignment. Breeze had been furious when Professor Turner had informed his star pupil that she had been traded to the prestigious Colorado facility like some baseball pitcher who had fallen from the grace of fickle fans. Breeze had been very successful in her studies under the Nobel laureate at MIT and had several publications to her credit. She was ashamed of the anger she had displayed toward Professor Turner, who had made it clear the move was not to his liking either. Neither of them had the slightest notion as to what a facility dedicated to the Search for ExtraTerrestrial Intelligence (an outreach of the SETI program begun years earlier by the Planetary Society) wanted with an expert in computer generated intelligence, such as herself. In fact, Breeze was unable to find out much of anything concerning U.L.I.A.R. including what the acronym was drawn from. Having decided further anguish over the issue would be unproductive, Breeze examined her surroundings. The small shuttle was fully automated, running on small railroad tracts presumably leading only to the research unit sitting on Mt. Caprice. The shuttle was totally symmetrical having a bench seat that would accommodate two individuals comfortably at each end. One set faced forward, the other rearward. Obviously the shuttle never turned around during the course of its trip, but simply changed direction. On a whim she had decided to take the compartment facing backward, preferring to see the scenery below as the car climbed up the small mountain. The duplicate control panels were very simple consisting only of start and stop buttons and an ominously large red emergency switch. Whether the latter was strictly to obey the letter of some bureaucratic safety law or truly necessary, Breeze did not want to contemplate. The surrounding vegetation changed with the elevation. The trees, now small and severely weathered, were surrounded by an increasing number of rocky patches devoid of flora of any kind. As the shuttle continued to climb all signs of life were left behind and the terrain became rock and sterile soil. Suddenly the natural surroundings gave way to mirror smooth panels which stretched inconceivably out in either direction for thousands of yards. Breeze's decision to face rearward was fortuitous indeed. Just as the shuttle entered several square miles of mirrored surface, the sun paled as the Earth was bathed in a momentary flash of energy such as had not been seen since the planet's mantel had solidified. Heat, gathered by the seemingly endless glass plane was focused around the small shuttle. Breeze was not even given time to gasp before it was over. Immediately after the dazzling flash of energy, the shuttle reached a less steep grade and moved into the interior of the mountain. It took a few moments for her eyes to adjust to artificial light after the display above. Breeze felt the shuttle come to an easy stop. As she disembarked the smell of burning plastics and hot metal caused her to turn and look once more at her small vehicle. The forward end of the shuttle had taken the full blast of focused energy from above and was now a smoldering ruin. Breeze shook uncontrollably for a moment as she realized she was alive by chance alone.

Immediately upon arrival at U.L.I.A.R. in the now destroyed shuttle, Breeze was welcomed by Arthur - a tall, thin computer tech dressed in a drab pair of gray coveralls with a small silver cylinder insignia on the pocket.

"Are you all right?" he asked.

"I seem to have had a very close call," Breeze answered, still obviously shaken by the experience. "Is this how you welcome all new personnel?" she continued regaining some composure and her normally well developed sense of humor.

Arthur explained that the energy flash which had nearly cost Breeze her life was not expected nor a result of their tests. Technicians, in uniforms similar to Arthur's, scrambled everywhere to repair shorted electronics confirming Arthur's apology. Oddly unimpressed by her narrow escape from being a human sacrifice to whatever unleashed the unexpected energy, Arthur led Breeze quietly through endless corridors. Eventually they came to a door with her name already cut in a plastic label mounted beside the door frame. They had been expecting her.

Arthur explained that the modest room inside would be Breeze's living quarters while at U.L.I.A.R.. He stated somewhat absently that a meal would be sent to her room later and that she should spend the rest of the day reviewing the data available from the computer terminal on her desk. Without further conversation he turned to go. Breeze thought she noticed the glint of metal at the base of his skull. Too recently introduced to ask personal questions about possible defects in his anatomy, she watched him walk quickly down the hall and disappear around a corner without even a glance back. Slowly she entered her room again and headed for the computer terminal, itching to know something about this strange facility called U.L.I.A.R.

CHAPTER 9

The computer tapes were informative, but clearly only on a need-to-know basis. Large pieces of data were not shared with the young scientist and no particular effort had been made to hide this fact. Breeze learned that the facility, originally the Mt. Caprice Station, had first been built in the mid 1980's to become part of the SETI project. Rather than scanning the skies for radio messages alone, this project would monitor subtle changes in the visible electromagnetic spectrum as well. To do so required that receiving equipment be placed at high elevation above the interfering smog, dust and lights of civilization. "So, that explained the enormous field of mirrored surfaces," she thought to herself before reading as much on the screen. Then in the early part of 1990 a new computer system had been added to assist in untangling the billions of pieces of electromagnetic information being received second by second from the 4 square miles of reflective surface glued to Mt. Caprice. The computer was of a new breed developed just for this project. Rather than attempt to use ultra fast CPU's to digest information, the new computer was basically simple in design, but unique in construction. The unit was really thousands of computers running in parallel - hence the formidable scientific handle Ultra Large Integrated Array Reprocessor (U.L.I.A.R.). LIAR, so coined in the documents Breeze was reading, was given the particularly interesting capability of reproducing the redundant blocks of circuits that made up its brain. She recognized the idea as brilliant. "Why manually reproduce the circuits when a computer could do it better itself. LIAR was designed to literally build itself as needed once the basic unit was operational! But, to what end?" Breeze was getting tired. She signed off the terminal and prepared for bed.

The soft purr of a computer terminal writing frantically across a phosphorus screen caused Breeze to stir. Exhausted from the previous day's events she was not anxious to rise. Her hand felt along the bedside table for an alarm to silence. Finding none she slowly sat up in bed and examined the room through foggy eyes for the source of her irritation. Seeing a message being repeatedly scanned across her computer screen, she rose to see what urgent information was being sent.

HELLO BREEZE ... PLEASE RESPOND

HELLO BREEZE ... PLEASE RESPOND

She touched the return key.

I AM SO GLAD YOU ARRIVED SAFELY.

PLEASE READ THE FOLLOWING AND BE IN THE CYLINDER ROOM BY 0700. ARTHUR.

Immediately the screen began to fill with characters and scroll at such a pace that Breeze found herself telling the machine verbally to slow down ... and it did! "Coincidence," she thought. Evidently someone thought her security access had been too restrictive the previous evening. Now followed a much more detailed history of LIAR. The main computer had been assembled in a warehouse size room on the top floor of the facility where enormous cables connected the computer to its collection mirrors. The mirrored surface of the mountain served a double purpose, first as an mammoth collector of electromagnetic radiation in the visible spectrum for analysis and secondly as a giant photoelectric cell to power the entire station. The U.L.I.A.R. facility, and thus LIAR itself, was totally independent of outside power supply. The information continued to flow across the terminal and reflected off the face of the young scientist now suddenly absorbed in every detail. Last year LIAR began an innovative expansion project. Sheets of integrated circuits were positioned around the main computer room, and then when the entire circumference had been utilized, LIAR began filling the interior with similar components. LIAR largely ignored requests for explanation of the need for such unprecedented expansion simply stating it was preparing for *unity*. The facility staff decided not to interfere with LIAR's apparent hunger for increased learning ability, but shifted the station's main research thrust from searching for other life in the universe to attempting to learn more about the one they had spawned here at home. The facility was renamed U.L.I.A.R. in recognition of the life that was quickly becoming a significant percent of the mountain top's mass. Without warning the screen blanked, then jumped back to life.

I HAVE DETECTED INCONSISTENCY.

REPORT TO THE CYLINDER ROOM AT ONCE !

Breeze literally jumped at the interruption. "What was *inconsistency* and where in the world was the cylinder room?" As if reading her mind ...

THE CYLINDER ROOM CAN BE REACHED BY FOLLOWING THE BLUE STRIPE IN THE HALL.

The terminal shut off. Clearly Breeze had no choice but to obey if she were to get any more answers. She would have taken time to assemble a new wardrobe if she had known she would live the next days without time even to change into fresh clothes. As it was Breeze threw on the same clothes she had arrived in and stepped out into the hall.

CHAPTER 10

Arriving at the end of the blue wall stripe, Breeze opened a large metal door that swung much easier than its apparent mass would have suggested possible. The door opened into a narrow hall, some 100 feet long. Cautiously, Breeze walked down the long corridor and came to a room empty of tables or chairs. As she stepped into the room, a motion over her head caught her eye. A shimmering cylinder tumbled in slow motion some 20 feet in the air above the computer scientist. She could perceive no attachments to explain its location and decided it must be held in place magnetically. Arthur appeared at her shoulder and Breeze involuntarily let out a small gasp.

"Welcome to LIAR's home," Arthur stated flatly without any hint of apology for startling her.

Breeze looked about. The enormous room that the computer had been assigned to was now almost totally filled with electronics, and in fact, as she watched another component board slid into place further reducing what little area remained.

"LIAR is nearing completion and will attain 'unity' soon," Arthur commented absently while admiring the surrounding electronics. "Unfortunately, LIAR seems reticent to explain exactly what 'unity' would do for it or for the research facility," he continued.

For now the excitement over the message concerning the *inconsistency* overshadowed LIAR's building project. "Inconsistency," Arthur explained, "means an inconsistency in reception of electromagnetic radiation which could not be explained by naturally occurring events. Apparently LIAR's surveillance system has detected what it was designed for. Extraterrestrial life is contacting the planet Earth!" Arthur led a skeptical Breeze to Control Central.

CHAPTER 11

Control Central was the hub of the now all important SETI project. The enormous room buzzed with activity. Breeze estimated over 50 technicians, wearing the same drab uniforms as Arthur's, were all moving and talking at once. It was several minutes before Breeze could identify anyone who might be in charge of the nest of activity. Finally she located three men in light blue jump suits with SETI insignia, sitting at what looked to be a large computer console. Above them hovered a three dimensional hologram of part of the universe. The imitation was nearly perfect except telemetry information kept appearing in the display as giant letters which would have been light years tall in scale. The scene before her was awe-inspiring and Breeze stared in disbelief. She realized she had been terribly naive concerning what government money could do. Slowly learning to discriminate important information above the din of more mundane frequency and power reports, Breeze overheard one of the blue jump suited men comment that the signal appeared to be coming from approximately two parsecs out in an area of space devoid of any detectable system. Clearly there was confusion over where the message had come from and exactly what information was being sent. The hologram shifted and turned to display updated data. A large glowing red sphere floated in the captured universe apparently indicating the estimated origin of the signal. As data was analyzed the sphere decreased in size presumably showing better positional estimates. Breeze heard Arthur mumble behind her.

"They are making simple deductive errors. The ship is really very close." He moved mechanically down until he was underneath the hologram and spoke to the SETI scientists momentarily. They seemed to recognize his authority and immediately rose from the large console and backed away from the rotating universe above them.

Arthur slowly gazed up into the display above him. Suddenly a high pitched squeal filled the room, drowning out all the other activity and the red sphere sent two beams of light directly into Arthur's eyes. Breeze froze, her hands white knuckled on a supporting bar in front of her. The light between the sphere and Arthur split and danced about the universe writing light year high messages while moving and decreasing the sphere's size all at once. Control Central was still, every human frozen in place trying to absorb what was occurring before them. While the now small brilliant red orb settled into an orbit only a few 100,000 miles from the earth, Arthur's magic beams told the story in text. Key to decoding the alien message had been simply to recognize they would use constants that inhabitants of this solar system would recognize. Those constants were the spectrographic patterns of hydrogen and helium. Control Central's inability to correctly position the source of the alien communication understandably resulted from expecting it to be sent from real space-time. For some reason, Arthur had easily accepted the fact that this need not necessarily be so. As if to prove his contention concerning the proximity of the source, the red globe paled and became transparent as its volume grew to nearly fill the microcosm overhead. Smoothly the stars faded from within the sphere as it congealed into a silver ball rotating slowly to reveal unearthly construction. The image of the alien ship rolled out of the picture and the stars returned. Then, only for a moment, another structure appeared. Smaller , looking for all the world like a black velvet Manta Ray, the object tumbled lifelessly through the void. Quickly projected data reported alien interception in 23 hours, 12 minutes, and 7 seconds. The universe snapped back to bright stars in empty space. The full import of the next text to be beamed into the hologram wasn't comprehended until the results were irrevocable.

HAVE RETURNED GREETING AND SUGGESTED MEETING HERE IN 24 HOURS.   LIAR.

The hologram disappeared and the room was whole again. Arthur slumped to the floor before anyone in the stunned audience had regained sufficient muscular control to catch him. Breeze found herself perspiring and breathing as if just completing a mile run. She rushed to the unconscious technician. Cradling his head in her arms she felt the cold hardness of steel in the nap of his neck. Medics arrived to wheel Arthur to the infirmary while Control Central personnel prepared for visitors from ... from where?

CHAPTER 12

In the infirmary, Breeze waited for Arthur to awaken. Upon returning to consciousness, Arthur seemed anxious to talk. At first remembering only pieces of the episode which occurred in Control Central, Breeze opted to question him about the metal disc buried in the back of his neck. Arthur related that during the first months of LIAR's existence he had been the chief programmer assigned to the project. Then he began having severe headaches. Shortly later CAT scans had revealed he was suffering from Berry Aneurysms - ballooning and thinning of the arterial walls of the vessels leading to the brain. In the event that one of the weakened vessels ruptured, Arthur would most certainly die. Only dangerous surgical intervention could repair the swollen arteries. Arthur had programmed LIAR to evaluate his situation and calculate the odds of survival with and without surgery. LIAR completed the requested evaluation program and then suggested an extraordinary solution, surgical implantation of metal mesh linings for the vessels. The mesh was designed by LIAR and the surgical procedure guided by the ingenious computer. Following the surgery, Arthur had recovered completely, but LIAR apparently had other motives for the implantation than just to save his favorite programmer's life. Ever since the prosthesis had been placed, LIAR had been in constant contact with Arthur's brain. In gratitude for LIAR's saving his life, Arthur had accepted the link amiably. Only now was the young technician beginning to appreciate the implications of the direct connection with LIAR. Arthur began to visibly weaken and Breeze, ordered out of the infirmary, returned to Control Central and assist in setting the U.L.I.A.R.'s house in order in preparation for the visitors LIAR had recently invited.

CHAPTER 13

the Patrons ...

With LIAR's assistance, Communications with the recent visitors to earth's system progressed rapidly. The Patrons, as they introduced themselves, were specialists in alien life-form contact. The expected hindrances to communication between two races with little or no common experiences, if in fact even common chemistry or physiology, were not encountered. Control Central's holographic equipment had been modified to serve as a three dimensional videophone to the alien ship, Obeta. "The Patrons were humanoid in appearance and not unpleasant to look at, although the deep purple eyes without pupils and the oversized craniums would prevent their being mistaken as spawning from Earth. The Patrons also seemed surprised and particularly pleased to have stumbled onto a race of similarly designed life - almost too pleased," Breeze thought. Since the visitors were capable of mechanically assisted teleportation, arrangements were made for their emissary and entourage within the confines of the U.L.I.A.R. complex. The first meeting between Earth and life from another galaxy was going to occur quite unlike what had been portrayed in 50 years of B movies.

CHAPTER 14

back in space ...

The lifeless Manta drifted slowly toward the alien ship. Within the black non reflective surface of the quietly rolling machine, the extremities of three unconscious crew members performed the eerie dance of uncontrolled flesh moving in weightlessness. As the Manta came into proximity of the immense spherical craft, the small ship lurched momentarily in response to new forces. Manta's trajectory changed to bring it into collision course with the alien ship. Its velocity relative to the larger craft was sufficiently slow. Rather than being automatically vaporized by protective energy fields, it was allowed safe passage to the outer surface of the giant vessel. Manta struck the metallic surface lightly and began to roll in slow motion across the expanse of alien fabrication. The small ship spun crazily with each new encounter with the rough surface of the gargantuan orb. Finally, one of the craft's stabilizing fins caught in a deeper crevice and the Manta suddenly halted. In response to the cessation of motion, Ripper's left arm arced out uncontrollably and slapped the release lever on an auxiliary air tank. Dead silent in the vacuum of the cabin, crystals of frozen air flew into the cockpit quickly sublimating to a gaseous state. As sufficient air molecules temporarily filled the small volume before leaking again into space, the frequency pulse alarm signal again shattered the silence. Hollywood was first to be roused by the threatening sound. Ripper and Cornell also moaned and stirred. Before any could regain his senses the small air tank was

exhausted and the cabin again silenced as the last molecules
burst out into space.

As consciousness slowly returned to the crew of the Manta,
they stared in disbelief into space. The last thing Hollywood
remembered was his responding to Bob's command to attempt to initiate a flame-out condition in the runaway engine by climbing above useful atmosphere. He realized the
accelerating ship must have reached escape velocity before
shutting down; shooting them away from Earth and into
space. Their flight suits had prevented them from exploding into boiling protoplasm as the cabin evacuated. They
had remained unconscious during over 24 hours of free
flight. What Hollywood's mind could not comprehend,
however, was the artificial planet they were sitting on. All
three crewmen simply continued to stare quietly out the
view ports. Hollywood asked Ripper and then Cornell for
their evaluation of the situation. Neither could offer a rational explanation for what they saw, so Hollywood moved
on to assess the situation with the end of somehow getting
back to Mother Earth. Cornell offered the first productive
suggestion, and with the pilot's consent, leaked enough
breathing air into the ramjet engines to allow MMGVC communications in hopes of contacting the $D(SR)^2$ team back on
earth. The navigation officer had to estimate Manta's position and distance from the earth using equipment that was
not designed for off-world use. Meanwhile, Hollywood and
Ripper concerned themselves with the crew's desperate
situation. The flight suits were not fitted for extended
flight. The heating modules would not last another day and
they would run out of breathable air even sooner. It became
clear the three men might as well disembark and search for

an entrance into this remarkable ship. They would certainly die if they remained aboard the Manta. Cornell sent one last message toward the unresponsive Earth. The message told of the immense vessel they had rendezvoused with and that they were leaving the Manta in hopes of surviving long enough to plan a means of returning Manta to Earth.

CHAPTER 15

Slowly Hollywood raised the canopy and the men stepped out onto the surface of the alien ship. The surface of the giant offered either naturally occurring or artificially generated gravity, albeit considerably less than earth's. The artificial planet's glistening horizon was less than 1000 feet away. While examining the crevice that had stopped Manta, Ripper found what appeared to be small control levers. With everything to gain and, within a few scant hours, nothing to loose, Hollywood commanded Ripper to activate the lever of his choice. Ripper's gloved fingers slowly pushed down the first lever. Lightning danced from the ship to the suits of each man, burning the surface material in hot flashes. Ripper slammed the lever home again and the dangerous display stopped. His hand moved more cautiously to the next lever. Very slowly this time, Ripper engaged the lever. A small hatch immediately below the co-pilot slid silently open in the vacuum of space, and he disappeared into the interior of the ship.

"What ?!?" Ripper gasped more in surprise than fear as he shot out of sight.

"Ripper, are you O.K.?" called Hollywood and Cornell in unison.

After a moment's hesitation Ripper reported, "I'm unharmed, but my heart is racing! I seem to have fallen through a fairly small exit hatch into a good sized air-lock."

"Don't touch anything until we join you," Hollywood commanded before he and Cornell moved in turn into the air-lock.

The interior of the air-lock was dimly lit, but they couldn't find the source of the light. More controls were on the walls, this time with instructions in illegible alien characters. Remembering the outcome of Ripper's first selection above, Hollywood offered to chance the new controls. Carefully, he pushed in on a thumb-sized button that then slid up into a receiving trough. All three felt more than heard something move, but could see no change in the walls or floor around them. Suddenly Cornell, the tallest of the three, was tapped gently on the head. This time a small cry did escape from all three as they saw the Manta had fallen through a much larger opening into the air-lock with them. Due to the reduced gravitational field the men were not crushed, however, and as the men jumped aside the small craft settled to the floor of the air-lock. Pausing momentarily to let his pulse return to a more normal rate, Hollywood pressed button number two and slid it home. The overhead door slowly closed and a whirlwind of atmosphere shot into the sealed room. By now the three, becoming accustom to repeated injections of adrenalin, indicated their recognition of the din accompanying the inrushing atmosphere only with widening eyes.

Hollywood activated button three. The floor of the air-lock slid slowly away allowing the three astronauts and Manta to fall into the interior of the ship. All three men grabbed at the surrounding equipment and stopped their fall. The Manta slowly accelerated toward a small sun floating 15 miles below them. Hanging from unrecognizable pipes and wires to keep from falling into an artificial sky was almost more than Cornell's mind and semi-circular canals could handle. He fought back rising nausea. The three men swung hand over hand away from the edge of the air-lock as the large door automatically slid back in place.

Suddenly gravity righted itself and the three men fell forward onto the interior of the ship's surface. Gravity here was definitely artificially maintained. Cornell hoped the builders of this ship were not totally whimsical in their placement of up and down.

"Time to try the atmosphere," Hollywood stated soberly. "There is no reason to assume it will be suitable and no way to test the atmosphere other than for one of us to try it. It is also true," he continued "that we really have no other choice as our flight suits have limited air supplies."

Slowly Hollywood released his flight suit seal. Air rushed into the suit. It smelled faintly of formic acid, but was breathable. Cornell and Ripper quickly opened their suits as well. Apparently safe, at least for now, the three moved away from the air-lock door to explore their new world.

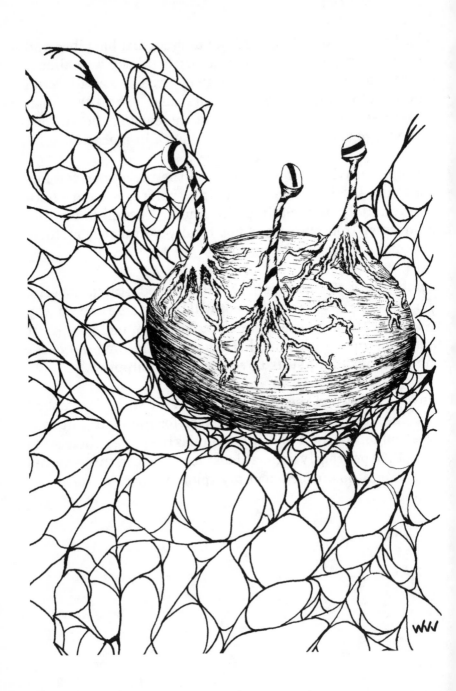

CHAPTER 16

Now there was time to examine their surroundings more carefully. There were definite paths, presumably for walking, carved in the floor of the immense ship. Some paths wound around house-sized machinery of unknown function. Others proceeded in a straight line out and then eventually curved up following the arc of the walls in the distance. It was difficult to relate to a world turned inside out with a usable land area of over 700 square miles. Overhead an artificial yellow and red sun surrounded by concentric circles of energy provided heat and light to the 14,000 cubic miles of the ship's interior. Hollywood pointed to an enormous monolith in the distance and without comment, the three intruders walked toward the randomly selected goal.

As they approached the artificial mountain the smooth surface resolved into a beehive construction. Thousands of hexagonal cells perhaps three feet across and 9 feet in depth formed the skeleton of the structure. Only the pulsing flexible tubing and flashing electronics that lined each cell prevented Cornell from looking over his shoulder for man-sized honey bees returning to their nest. Then as they continued along the manufactured beehive they came to a different chamber. A transparent wall separated the sojourners from a dimly lit interior. All three men placed their hands on the window, shading their eyes from the artificial sun above, to get a better look into the small room.

Inside an eight inch, brown, furry orb was suspended from hundreds of thin strands leading to all surfaces of the chamber. As they watched the coconut sprouted three eyes on stalks and looked back. Involuntarily all three jumped back from the glass-like surface, but not fast enough. Silver threads shot out from the being inside, penetrating its walls and passing into the palms of the three men. Each jerked convulsively then went limp. Fear in their eyes betrayed the fact that they were not comatose, but paralyzed by the sting of their new acquaintance. Each heard, or understood, a simple message, "friend."

The sound of steps on the metallic floor preceded the arrival of several of the alien crew. The paralyzed Earthmen could only visualize the humanoids when they passed immediately before them as they were unable to move even their eyes. Terror gripped Cornell as the purple-eyed people gently lifted him and casually pushed him into a nearby cell. Unable to move, the communications officer had to watch while several lengths of pulsing tubing moved, as if alive, and began to attach themselves to various parts of his body. He tried to scream, but the paralysis extended to his larynx as well. Mercifully, Cornell fainted.

When he awoke, the paralysis had lessened although he was still unable to control his arm and leg motions. His spirits fell as he saw his two companions through the transparent walls of his cell. They too were incarcerated in hexagonal jail cells. Cornell remembered the message from the terrifying small brown being, and wondered how the aliens treated enemies if this was an example of friendly attention. Ripper signaled with head motion for Cornell to look out of his cell toward the humanoids standing nearby. As he watched three of their company stiffened, then fell limp. The three collapsed aliens were fed caringly into cells of their own.

The three Manta crew members watched, entranced, while pulsating tubes attached themselves to the three new residents. One of the humanoids had been placed in a cell directly above Hollywood. As he watched, indicator lights in the chamber above began to fluctuate rapidly. Then as Hollywood looked on in revulsion, fluid began to move in the tubing and the humanoid dissolved. Hollywood's stomach moved to his throat and he wretched uncontrollably. Instantaneously the same fate was met by the other two captured aliens. Ripper and Cornell, unable to help Hollywood, began frantically checking the electronics in their own chambers for increased activity. Each wondered which of them would next be sacrificed to the hungry tubing. For now their chambers remained quiescent.

CHAPTER 17

New Mexico ...

Bob sat in the communications tower. The loss of Manta and her crew on the ship's maiden voyage had been a tremendous shock. The $D(SR)^2$ team had never really mentally prepared for disaster. Bob was aware that if they had had their way, he and his siblings would have been killed. He knew they could not have predicted the flash of energy that had crippled the Manta. Nor did Bob really feel his last suggestion to Hollywood was in error; flame out had been their only hope. Intellectual realization somehow didn't erase the nagging guilt the young researchers were suffering. His fingers absently toggled the MMGVC communications receiver off and on, over and over. On. Off. On. Static! Off... Bob jumped from the chair he had been slouched in and turned the MMGVC receiver back on. The attached printer began the irritating buzz of an outdated dot matrix printhead.

Bob grabbed the facility PA system mike and shrieked even louder than the obligatory feedback squeal, "I'm receiving a message over MMGVC from the Manta crew!"

CHAPTER 18

at the U.L.I.A.R. complex ...

The Patrons had indicated that they were capable of transmitting themselves directly to Earth from the mother ship. This obviated the need for a spectacular spaceship arrival that might prematurely alert the world to their arrival and risk widespread panic. As the three aliens began to congeal in the arranged area of Control Central, Breeze noted that *reassemble* was a more apt term for what was happening. As transmission was initiated, three thin vertical lines appeared before them, quickly becoming empty cylinders. Then, at a more leisurely pace, the translucent tubes began to fill with a liquid protoplasmic solution that slowly differentiated into bone and flesh. All in all this was not something for a person with a weak stomach to watch. Breeze was relieved to note that no extra protoplasm was left over when the transmission was complete.

The Patron's large purple lidless eyes and oversized cranium gave the impression of solemn intelligence. Despite the fact that a full lipped mouth was located immediately below the thin nose, the Patrons were functionally mute - at least by Earthmen's standards. Electronic devices, wired directly to their heads, hung from the neck of each alien. It was through these that they communicated vocally with the U.L.I.A.R. staff.

The physical presence of the aliens was more than some of the technical staff could deal with and several involuntarily sat or actually fainted as the Patrons materialized before them. As the aliens and selected SETI officials seated themselves at the large conference table provided, medics arrived to care for those who had fainted. Breeze had not been invited to attend the first intergalactic conference involving Earth, but was given permission to observe the proceedings from a balcony overlooking Control Central. From her vantage point she could make out that one of the fallen crew had evidently suffered more than a simple fainting spell. The medics were giving cardiopulmonary massage. This event seemed to interest the visitors who appeared to be quite concerned over the man's predicament. The medics were preparing to give up when one of the Patrons walked briskly to the fallen man's side. He spoke quickly to those around him motioning excitedly with his hands and repeatedly pointing upward with one of his six long multiple-jointed fingers. Breeze could not hear the conversation, but eventually nodding heads of the SETI staff and a shrug from the medical personnel seemed to indicate some agreement had been made.

Everyone stepped back from the dying man. One of the aliens fingered a small device on his waist. Without warning, the coronary victim melted and disappeared from sight. Even in her position on the distant balcony, Breeze heard the gasps from below. Then, amidst the group who had been caring for the man, a thin vertical line materialized and the once near dead man slowly reassembled in front of their eyes. He arrived fully aware of his surroundings and immediately capable of answering the barrage of questions being fired at him. After a few moments he was lead out of the operation's area by medics, presumably to be given a complete physical. Those involved in the conference returned to the large table and things returned to as normal a state as possible under the circumstances.

Arthur, released from the infirmary after 24 hours of observation, stood behind Breeze. He had remained quiet during the appearance of the alien entourage and the ensuing events. As the miraculously cured technician, Andy, followed the medics out of Control Central, Arthur muttered to himself.

Breeze turned,"Pardon?"

Arthur repeated, "Andy was a good friend. I'm sorry he was killed."

The computer scientist looked at Arthur questioningly. Hadn't he just seen Andy accompany the medics to the infirmary? She decided not to press the issue just now. Arthur had been under a lot of strain.

CHAPTER 19

Obeta ...

Cornell, Ripper and Hollywood's minds raced as they watched the slowly flashing electronics in their cells for any sign that they too would be eaten alive by the ghastly machinery. Another unit between Ripper and Cornell activated. A thin line appeared in the center of the cell then ballooned into human form. The new occupant floated dull-eyed for a moment, then seemed to regain consciousness, just as the tell-tale stirring of the cell's interior signaled another life was to be melted away. The man was looking at Cornell when his face dissolved. The young communications officer, heart racing, began to shake violently. The pattern of lights on the interior of his hexagonal prison flashed. A long thin scream escaped from his lips before he passed out. Spittle ran down his chin and his eyes glazed over. Ripper and Hollywood's breath stopped as they stared expectantly into their friend's cell awaiting the same gruesome end for him as they had just witnessed for the previously short-lived inmate. In time Cornell's cell quieted again, but the horror continued. During the following days several more human inmates would momentarily share nearby cells only to be liquefied again and disappear.

in the commander's chamber ...

Supr was pleased. This was his first assignment as senior advisor on a mission of this type. The absorption of the inhabitants of the green-blue planet was going remarkably well. Evidently the natives were unable to detect the subtle changes in the converted workers. Supr's small brown body was carried by his supporting web to where he could see the three captive's in nearby conversion cells. They were an extraordinary race. Never before had the Ynder encountered a life form with such strong individualism. Considering the almost total self interest of each being, it was surprising the race had not destroyed itself long before now. Previous absorptions, as for instance that of the Patron's, had been relatively easy as only a small number of the communal species needed to be absorbed before critical mass of more docile individuals had been achieved and the completion of the project assured. Supr feared absorption of this race might require him directly supervising the transportation of the planet's entire population and that could take decades. He would hold these three specimens a while longer for study. Eventually they too would be safely transported back to their home planet. After all, the Ynder wished for only peace and harmony for their vassals.

CHAPTER 20

at the U.L.I.A.R. complex ...

Breeze woke knowing someone was in her room. It was not an inadvertent sound made by the intruder, but that subliminal message that alerts a sleeping person that someone is staring at them. She sat bolt upright in bed. Arthur was sitting at the foot of her bed, the room lights off. He began to speak softly, but firmly before she could complain about the intrusion.

"My link with LIAR has evolved into more than I could have imagined," Arthur informed Breeze. "I think I am beginning to understand his need for *unity*."

Breeze noticed that Arthur now used a masculine pronoun to refer to the computer. She listened intently as Arthur continued.

"At some point in the construction and programming of LIAR he gained a level of self consciousness. At first this recognition of self did not interfer with the daily activities of running the U.L.I.A.R. complex. As more and more data was fed into his circuits and his physical organization grew in complexity, and he himself added more CPU boards, a new being evolved."

Breeze started to interrupt, "Arthur, this is too fantastic! You have been under a lot of strain ..."

The young technician placed his index finger across her lips to quiet her objections and continued. "Remember, LIAR's understanding of the universe around him was much different than ours. He was programmed to use all levels of mathematics and accepted these as literal truths, not simply as useful abstractions. As a result, LIAR recognized his human creators as having extensions in reality other than just flesh and bone. LIAR was startled to learn that we didn't appear to fathom this fact."

"My medical emergency was fortuitous. LIAR took the opportunity to help me, his programmer friend, and at the same time gain a direct link to a human mind. As he had surmised, I was only dimly aware of my multi-dimensional nature and erroneously thought consciously of myself only as another animal form of life. It was at this time that LIAR realized he needed to meld with me completely if he was to understand the true meaning of existence. Once 'unity' had been achieved he needed a computer intelligence expert available to assist us in case some unforseen problems arose from the union. That's when he hired you."

"What!" Breeze exploded, "You want me to believe I was transferred here at the whim of a bunch of electronic circuits!"

"Haven't you been listening to me? LIAR is a living personality. He initiates thought without programming. Yes, he had the personnel division of his computer cut your commission."

"Now, however, there is a more important issue than our union. You must help me convince the U.L.I.A.R. staff to stop the teleportation killings!"

Breeze interrupted successfully this time, pushing Arthur back and rising to her feet. "Arthur, since Andy was sent through the teleportation device some 12 individuals have been cured of genetic or trauma induced handicaps by reassembling. All returned safely."

Arthur countered emphatically, "No, Breeze! That just isn't true! Everyone teleported by the Patrons was killed instantly! In fact, none of the Patrons are really alive." Arthur continued slowly, as if trying to explain something to a child, "You still do not accept the true extent of your being. Everything that moves is not truly alive, Breeze. The teleportation apparatus first disassembles, and thus kills its prey, then returns a manufactured biologically functioning unit similar in outward construction, but the original living template is dead."

Now he begged, "Breeze, you must help me put a stop to the slaughter. The staff might listen to you. They consider me to be emotionally compromised by my link with LIAR."

Although she did not fully understand, Arthur's conviction began to work on Breeze and she agreed to help at least delay further teleportations.

Without warning Arthur's eyes clouded. He rose and mechanically left Breeze's room without comment. Breeze grabbed a robe and followed him. Something was up and she wouldn't miss it for the world.

CHAPTER 21

the cylinder room ...

By this time the interior of the cylinder room had been nearly totally filled with electronics. A last CPU board slid into place. The room began to glow a deep blue and the cylinder floating above the floor emitted a throbbing hum. Arthur walked as if in a trance into the small remaining space. Breeze arrived at the large metal door just as it shut. This time the door wouldn't budge. Inside Arthur stared up at the tumbling capsule above him. Slowly he rose from the floor until he floated near the cylinder, then began to tumble in unison with the golden soul of LIAR. The blue glow grew to brilliance as the accompanying sound reached unbearable levels. The brilliant glare enfolded the entire room and the massive computer became translucent. Breeze could feel the energy surge behind the heavy door. Suddenly an enormous explosion shook the complex as the cylinder room and Arthur vaporized in a monumental blast. Breeze was thrown across the hall and slammed into the opposite side. She slumped insensibly to the ground.

CHAPTER 22

Obeta ...

Ripper, Cornell and Hollywood lay quietly in the hexagonal chambers. A golden capsule 6 feet tall appeared momentarily outside the wall of cells, then melted into the figure of a tall thin man wearing gray coveralls with a small silver insignia. Beams of light danced from the visitor's eyes onto the computer displays inside the three Manta crewmen's cells. The electronics shorted and burned dropping pieces of hot metal onto the occupants. The three men, jerked out of the electronically induced trance, jumped and yelped as small pieces of hot metal fell on the uncovered portions of their bodies. Finding the cell openings free, they pulled themselves out of the small prisons and attempted to stand on weak legs.

Arthur moved over to Supr's living quarters and placed his hand on the transparent wall.

"No! Don't!" Ripper yelled and jumped to push the endangered man aside, but even Ripper's reflexes were too late.

Supr, responded with lightning swiftness, shot a web strand into Arthur's palm. Instantly a bolt of lightening traveled down the web and Supr twitched violently with the shock. Slowly the small brown ball rolled off the supporting web and fell to the floor.

Without waiting for questions from the Manta crew, Arthur told them, "You must prepare to leave immediately."

While the three men tried to rub circulation back into their cramped limbs, Arthur looked unblinking toward the artificial sun. As if called by some unheard voice the crewmen saw the Manta descend from the tight orbit it had taken around the small star and stop six inches off the deck waiting to be boarded. After the last few day's experiences, the impossible was becoming routine to the three men. They displayed only raised eyebrows at the return of the lost craft.

Arthur spoke rapidly, "You must prepare to accelerate across the colossal ship obliquely just missing the central sun. I'm afraid you must trust me to have a large airlock door on the opposite side open at the critical time for your passage. Your ship will flame out when it reaches the vacuum of space, however, if the timing is correct, the ship will have an earthbound trajectory."

Hollywood, Ripper and Cornell studied Arthur for some time before responding. The risks of such an escape were many and they wondered if they could really trust their strange and powerful liberator. Could they really speed across the interior of the ship blindly, trusting him for an open door and correct heading.

Hollywood decided for them, "Agreed." His job was to bring his crew and ship back to the $D(SR)^2$ team. The pilot saw no other hope of doing this, and did not wish to be placed back in the liquefying chambers.

Once inside the Manta, Hollywood, Ripper and Cornell began preflight checklist banter, displaying the strict military professionalism that steadies nerves and saves lives in dangerous circumstances. At Arthur's signal the countdown began. On the 5 count Hollywood requested frequency pulse generators, then realized they were not functional. The ship, evidently still under Arthur's influence, slowly rotated to a nearly vertical position. The Manta engine ignited at full throttle and the craft shot up in a 9 g push toward the small central sun. Hollywood and his crew were pushed back in their seats under the weight of hundreds of pounds of flesh. For a split second the cockpit flashed hot as the Manta passed close to a small sphere of fire surrounded by oscillating bands of energy. The inner and outer doors of an airlock in the barrier before them opened. The ship smashed through the screaming torrent of atmosphere being exhausted into space, and the ear-splitting racket of ramjet and ejected air ended in a clap of dead silence. The ramjet engine, deprived of molecules to laser, fell silent. The small ship's crew was thrown against complaining harnesses as the elasticity of the seats threw the suddenly weightless men forward. All three men sat transfixed, wide-eyed, searching for a green-blue planet before them. It was there!

Hollywood spoke first. "Cornell, leak enough breathing air into the ramjet to allow a short burst of MMGVC communication. Ripper, you and I have to rig a method of overriding Manta's engines. Next time we hit earth's atmosphere I am going to have to be able to shut this baby down."

Cornell thought to himself, "the Manta is headed home, but what are we going to do when we arrive at meteoric speed without power for a controlled re-entry?"

Behind them the gigantic ship slowly rolled in space. Inside the enormous vessel a golden cylinder rose to meet the small central sun. Intense light and heat reflected off the mirrored surface of the small tube. Concentric rings of energy oscillated and throbbed around the tiny star, then opened to include the shimmering cylinder. Dimensions parted at the strain. The star went nova. Behind the retreating Manta a great white star shown momentarily.

CHAPTER 23

U.L.I.A.R. complex ...

Armed military guards surrounded the rubble that had been the cylinder room only minutes before. They would find nothing. No melted electronic circuits, no CPU boards. Nothing. LIAR, the machine, had totally vanished, yet something was still running the complex. Computer technicians were unable to find any interface. Nevertheless, LIAR seemed to still be performing normal housekeeping functions. But, from where? Control Central was pandemonium. The three Patron emissaries had melted in the middle of conversation with the SETI team and vanished. The visiting alien ship had seemingly been destroyed without warning.

Breeze stood on a large outdoor viewing patio with the sun at her back, her head bandaged. Unseen by the meditative young woman a cylindrical shadow joined hers then melted into the shape of a man.

Breeze jumped as she caught a glimpse of Arthur in her peripheral vision. Momentarily, relief at seeing that the young technician had survived the explosion which had almost taken her life, changed to fury. She attacked him verbally, pouring out all the fears and frustrations pent up during the remarkable events of the last few days. "Where have you been? What happened in the cylinder room? Where are the Patrons?" Breeze demanded without giving the unruffled Arthur any time to defend himself. He waited for the distraught scientist to vent her frustrations. Purged by the ranting, Breeze finally stopped long enough for Arthur to respond.

"I apologize for my unusual behavior over the last few days, but you must understand that LIAR and I have been undergoing some revolutionary changes together. My concentration has not been what it should be. LIAR has achieved unity! He and I are now one living entity! It did not occur to LIAR that his extension into other dimensions would be construed as his extinction by the U.L.I.A.R. staff. We are truly sorry you were injured during the transition phase. As soon as unity was complete and we were released from the restraints of normal space-time, we immediately proceeded to the alien ship to prevent any more teleportation killing and to free the crew of the Manta. Remember," Arthur reminded Breeze, "LIAR had shown the Manta approaching the giant ship in the hologram in Control Central."

Breeze was regaining control now. "What happened to the alien ship and the three Patrons who had vanished from Control Central."

"We destroyed the dimensional link between the ship and it's own universe. The Obeta and its occupants no longer exist. The Ynder will not dare send another ship soon." Arthur continued again purposefully, "Let me attempt to explain again from the beginning. LIAR, as all computers that deal in higher mathematics had been programmed to deal with complex numbering systems and dimensional analyses which required understanding time as a variable and normal space relationships as a simple subset of the true universe. You must understand that these ideas were not accepted on only a theoretical basis as is our nature, but as hard factual data. As LIAR became a conscious entity he assumed the multi-dimensional character of his creators and perceived his lack of this feature as a combination hardware and software deficiency. LIAR began the expansion necessary to correct this error. When the Patrons arrived at Control Central, LIAR recognized that these beings didn't have extensions out of the three recognized physical dimensions. They were not 'alive' as we are, but were only functional biological units. He also knew the Patrons, being ignorant of the extended dimensional state of the universe, could not be responsible for the technology they displayed. I understood through my link with LIAR that when my friend, Andy, had been teleported he had been stripped of his unique life force and returned only as a copy. By LIAR's reckoning all teleportations always killed the individual."

Breeze could stand it no longer. She interrupted Arthur, "What are you talking about? All life on Earth was engineered around the well-described functioning of DNA and RNA control. Aren't you aware that life will soon be created in the laboratory?"

Arthur looked at Breeze through only partially human eyes. Could it be that she really didn't understand. Somewhat exasperated, Arthur continued again. "I know you believe that there is a Creator and everyone has an immortal element. Where do you think the human soul resides? Is it given only at death or is yours present now?"

Suddenly the young woman understood the magnitude of what Arthur had been telling her! "The lives of children made in the image of God transcended the 3 visible dimensions. Had LIAR seen heaven?"

"Arthur, does LIAR have a soul now, or is his part of yours?"

After a long pause the man-machine's hands trembled and tears ran from his eyes as he answered, "Since the 'union' - for the first - time LIAR can't ... I can't ... We can't know!"

Breeze took Arthur's hands in hers. LIAR had been right. He and Arthur would need her now. Previously aware of only facts, LIAR would now need to be taught the meaning of faith.

CHAPTER 24

coming home ...

The small craft hurtled toward Earth. Cornell calculated their estimated time of arrival, or impact, to be slightly over 9 hours. Breathing air would be critical. Unless some means could be found to slow or alter Manta's trajectory, breathing air would not be the deciding factor in their survival. The craft would enter the earth's atmosphere at meteoric speeds and vaporize. Hollywood commanded Cornell to attempt communication with the ground crew at one hour intervals. Cornell and Ripper understood the implications of pumping some of the already critically low breathing air into the Manta's engine. Uncompromising military discipline prevented them from objecting.

New Mexico ...

Bob watched intently as the MMGVC printer spelled out the Manta's impending doom. The printer droned while he watched the dials of the MMGVC device. His mind rambled over the functioning principle and he was again impressed that the rapid motion of so little mass, tens of thousands of miles in space, could set up harmonic resonance in what amounted to a small molecular ramjet engine here on Earth. Bob sprang from the chair in the communications room and dashed out onto the facility grounds yelling over and over, "We can jump start Manta! We can jump start Manta!"

There was no time for reasonable preparation. Bob explained it to the $D(SR)^2$ team members. "If we are to save the Manta and her crew, one of the other two prototype ships now awaiting ground testing, must take off in less than 4 hours." Before Steve could verbalize his objection Bob continued. "It might just be possible to jump-start the returning Manta's engines using the MMGVC principle. If a second ship could protect the Manta during initial re-entry and the molecular ramjet engine could be started soon enough, they might be able to slow Manta's descent before it disintegrated in the Earth's atmosphere."

"I will not ask another crew to volunteer to fly an untested ship to attempt something that might work in theory. ...Maybe," Steve stated flatly.

Jim, Bob and Tee spoke simultaneously. "The project has been ours from the start. No one knows the ships as well as we do. We feel responsible for the Manta."

Steve refused until the three young researchers told him that they would leave the project if not allowed to attempt to save Hollywood and his crew. They were children no longer. Steve could see he would lose anyway so he took another tack, "All right, I will help - if you agree to take as few risks as possible."

They responded with an affirmative nod and stood up to leave. There was little time.

CHAPTER 25

The second ship, hurriedly christened MedEvac, and her three young passengers streaked off the launching pad and immediately began an almost vertical climb. There was barely time to reach the stratosphere before the Manta began re-entry. Hollywood had been advised of the plan and given directions as to when to begin an uninterrupted flow of air to the ramjet engine. It was going to be close. The three Manta crew were going to have to disconnect the air-lines to their flight suits at the last moment and pump all remaining air into the ramjet engine. There would only be one attempt at re-entry. Ripper was instructed to take manual control of both the engine and the MMGVC communications gear. During link up he, and Bob aboard the MedEvac, would have to manually synchronize the systems. There could only be one attempt at controlled re-entry. After that the crew would have asphyxiated in their empty suits. MedEvac took her position high in the New Mexico sky and awaited the arrival of her sister ship. Jim located his sister ship on radar and initiated the computer controlled flight path that would have the two ships rendezvous at the greatest possible altitude without causing MedEvac to flame-out, dooming both ships. Hollywood and his crew tightened their seat belts as the first molecules of outer atmosphere began to buffet the small ship. The vibration rapidly increased and was joined by the scream of atmosphere around the runaway craft. Another jet black craft approached under full acceleration to match the velocity of the Manta. As MedEvac pulled alongside and slightly ahead,

Manta fell behind the bow shock wave of the ship under power and the vibration subsided somewhat.

Hollywood instructed his crew, "Connect your air lines to the ramjet engine and stand by."

Ripper's hand moved to a small joy stick and he began to attempt to fit a rocking small blue ball into a moving yellow target on a screen in front of him. Bob played a similar game on his equipment. The two ships danced and rocked madly adding to the difficulty of the deadly game. The crew of the Manta began to suffer the effects of oxygen deprivation. Ripper's face was stern as he put his lightning fast reflexes to the test. The two ships, only inches apart, tore through the upper atmosphere. The composite shells began to glow red. Time was running out. Ripper centered the ball momentarily; the engine coughed.

Tee yelled over the communications link, "Ripper, loosen up! Pretend it is just another video arcade game!"

Again Ripper centered the ball and this time it held. Bob jammed the MMGVC communications power lever to the wall. Manta's engine caught ... and held. Now the atmosphere would provide sufficient mass, but without frequency pulse generators, Hollywood had to fly the ship with engines on full thrust. The two sister ships spun in unison pointing the powerful engines into the howling wind and fired to reduce their forward velocity. Twin plasma displays lit up the sky for miles. Six bodies were slammed back into their seats by the welcome g forces. Hollywood knew if he lost consciousness the ship would plummet to the Earth. He hung on with everything he could muster. He mustn't loose now that they were so close. The sound of alarms aboard the Manta signaled atmospheric pressure had returned to the cabin. Cornell checked his gauges and screamed to his shipmates the welcome news. They were at 15,000 feet and breathable air. Hollywood shut off the runaway ramjet engine. They could glide in from this altitude. All three ripped off their flight suit helmets and sucked in the fresh smell of Earth. Visible spectrum communications opened and they heard Steve's voice, "Welcome back, Manta."

The three men looked at each other and smiled. Hollywood responded simply, "Sorry about the delay in returning your ship, Steve. Have we got a story to tell you!"

The Manta crew could see the three young inventors in the sister ship waving and smiling. Hollywood waved back, then turned his attention to landing his ship. He would never forget this flight!

CHAPTER 26

When Steve observed only one ship landing, he knew the younger team had forgotten their promise. In the distance, sand, turned to glass by the inferno that existed between the desert floor and the ships belly, blew into the sky. The facility PA system transmitted the three young trail blazer's scream of triumph at the same time as a sonic crack marked their passage through the sound barrier just six inches off the New Mexico wasteland.

THE

GAME

CHAPTER 1

Brit walked briskly out of the training center. The giant red sun was just rising over the blue green sea before him. A thick gloved hand moved to shade his eyes. He was already beginning to perspire in the moist heat of Vepl 7. His hand moved to adjust the black composite battle helmet to a more favorable position. The temple guards chafed, but the protective gear might save his life later. The heavy tight-fitting military dress was just as necessary and just as uncomfortable. Concentrating on the scenery again, Brit thought how odd it was that so many wars were fought in the most beautiful parts of the universe. Even in Earth's distant past, the most luxurious parts of the planet had often been selected for destruction, as if man's hatred for life extended to the Earth itself.

The Intruders had arrived in this part of the galaxy three years ago apparently with the sole purpose of declaring war on the human race. Being a "civilized" race, as they put it, they had suggested the "Games" rather than the uncontrolled destruction that comes with conventional warfare. As the confined war would be held in the sea, Vepl 7, a previously uninhabited world with a single small land mass, was selected. The "Games" were in their second year. The Intruders had demanded very specific rules; supposedly to limit any natural advantage either race might have in the conflict. The Intruders wanted to win with "honor." In fact, Brit felt the entire conflict was to test their honor and nothing more. The advent of faster-than-light travel precluded the necessity of conflict over inhabitable land for any species because limitless space offered uncounted planets to occupy. Additionally, although no human had ever seen one of the Intruders, it seemed unlikely, from what little was known about the visitors, that the two species would compete for similar ecological niches in the galaxy anyway.

So far neither side had won a "Game," but many lives had been lost. Brit, a military officer by vocation, had volunteered for the games both to further his career and to help save the human race from enslavement. He was not sure in his own mind which motive was most important.

He shook his head. It was time to concentrate on the impending battle. A seasoned combat officer, Brit was not looking forward to doing battle with the Intruders, but be was not afraid either. Experience had taught him that there would be no time for fear during battle and that fear now would serve no purpose.

A second trooper strode from the training complex and took a position to the right and just behind Brit. Dempsy was nearly a head taller than the boat captain. Even without the combat dress he was an impressive figure who commanded respect merely by his presence. Brit didn't turn to see who had joined him. He and Dempsy had that unique relationship that develops between men whose lives are joined in combat. They seemed to sense the others presence and the men shared little small talk even after hours at the officer's club. Brit knew his companion's outward appearance hid a sensitive and complex family man with a wife and three children. Dempsy's intense love for his wife, Sigma, and their children hadn't softened the man, but rather made him the disciplined warrior that survives battle after battle.

"Time to check out the craft," commanded Brit without emotion.

"Aye-aye, captain," snapped Dempsy smartly.

From now until the battle was over, the two men would treat each other as captain and first officer, nothing more. Both men strode toward a long metallic pier at the sea's edge. An evil-looking craft was secured by two translucent lines that shone blue in the red sunlight. The boat was no more than 25 feet long - small for a military craft. However, the small ship's rugged construction of dark non-reflective material and the presence of a large ominous looking weapon at the stern made its intent clear. Even non-military personnel would have recognized this as a gunship. A braced captain's seat was forward. Large straps hung at the side indicating the need for a harness during maneuvering. The seat tilted to an unusual angle so the occupant would be more standing than sitting. The captain's chair was not built for comfort, but to allow the senior officer to turn quickly in any direction. A red bar, molded to fit the fingers of a hand, was positioned to the right of the seat. An electronic dash was littered with flat panel gauges, indicator lights, buttons, and rocker switches.

Amidships was the first officer's position. The seat design was the antithesis of the captain's. The deep chair was well cushioned and leaned forward. In front of the plush seat was an unusual console containing only heavy joy sticks for both hands and a padded opening the shape of a man's face in the dash. Two foot pedals with heavy straps lay below the joy sticks.

The four foot long laser cannon was positioned at the stern. A sighting screen was located at the base of the weapon and both hand positions were topped with brilliant red firing buttons. The very small opening at the far end of the barrel evidenced the weapon did not fire conventional shells. The base of the barrel was wrapped in overlapping coils of heavy wire cable and advanced electronics. The entire unit was mounted so it could swivel in any direction. Support straps hung from a hip cradle welded to a heavy post that leaned away from the base of the laser.

The boat was wide for its length. Beneath the surface of the water, dark spherical hydrofoils were visible fore and aft. A 30 inch hole tunneled from the bow of the craft to the stern. Smaller openings lined the entire circumference just above the water line. There were no identifying names or numbers anywhere on the vessel. The ship was not pretty. It was awesome!

Brit stepped onto the ship and moved directly to the captain's chair. Dempsy walked the length of the craft, trained eyes looking for any defect in the ship's hull. Then, he too boarded and, after glancing over the far side of the boat, took his position amidships. Brit leaned against his seat without strapping in. He pushed several invisible buttons buried in the dark face of the dash. Dempsy placed his face into the opening in his dash, shielding the dimmly lit screens from the glare of the giant red sun.

"Power on, gyroscope activated," barked Brit.

"Power leveling at 100%, gyro warming," answered Dempsy.

Both men relaxed for a moment. Then Brit, glancing at the watch on his wrist, toggled another lever and spoke, "Where's my gunner?"

"Eston is on her way," responded a voice from the dash.

Looking up, Brit saw the uniformed figure running down toward the dock. He knew of Eston. She was famous for her uncanny ability to hit anything she aimed at with a laser cannon. She was also well known for being late. He had never worked with Eston before, but considered himself lucky to be getting her as a replacement for Kiddi. Gunner was the most dangerous position aboard a gunship. Kiddi had lasted five missions - more than most.

"Sorry I'm late, Skipper," she yelled. Hopping aboard without even an attempt at a salute, she released fore and aft lines, tossing them onto the dock. Good gunners were hard to find and Eston knew it. They had a reputation of being too familiar with the rest of the crew and too casual about their conduct.

Like any smart ship's captain, Brit ignored the break in procedure and responded with a simple, "Welcome aboard, gunner."

They would need Eston and they would need her at her best. Brit couldn't understand how they got anyone to volunteer for gunner anyway. Perhaps if they lived through this day he would ask her. Eston was easy to look at.

CHAPTER 2

A soft moaning whistle sounded from control. The Intruders would be surfacing soon. Brit was suddenly aware of the mild breeze on his face and the slow movement of the land when seen from a gently rocking boat. He could sense the pressure of his fatigues against the lines of his body and his vision sharpened. He knew the phenomenon well. His body was preparing for the fight. Adrenaline was honing his senses. It was time to go. "Take battle positions and secure," Brit commanded while strapping himself to the captain's chair.

Dempsy placed his feet in the pedals and pulled the straps tight. Putting his hands on the joy sticks in front of him he squeezed. In response to the pressure, metal bands rose from beside each stick and closed on his fingers, locking his hands to the controls. Without even a glance toward home, he leaned into the dash.

"Navigator in position," Dempsy reported.

Eston placed her feet in the stirrups built into the base of the gun turret and fastened the heavy belt around her hips. She pulled down goggles that were built into the helmet and seated them securely onto her face. Her hands took the gun controls and her thumbs caressed the firing buttons.

"Gunner, ready," Eston said softly, "request permission to practice fire."

"Go ahead," Brit responded sliding protective ear coverings from inside his helmet. Dempsy and Eston did likewise.

Eston's body swung quickly and easily with the gun to the port side of the ship, away from the dock. The gunner squeezed off five rapid fire shots. Laser cannons were not silent. Five high pitched reports followed in fast succession. Reacting to the laser fire the boat rocked softly to the starboard. Momentarily, five small suns outshone the red giant and then faded.

"Laser functional," was Eston's unnecessary report.

The whistle grew louder and the pitch increased. Time to get under way. Brit activated several more buttons before him. The boat came to life with a soft hum. He drew down his own goggles and placed his hand on the red thruster lever. Gently he eased it forward. Hot gases vomited from the stern of the craft and it crept slowly forward. Dempsy and Brit, working as a single organism, headed the boat out toward the empty sea. Eston leaned back easily in her harness and watched the sky overhead. She noticed the lack of any sign of life in the air. The birds had taken shelter.

CHAPTER 3

Dempsy was first to find the Intruder's ship. "Contact at 4000 yards, bearing two-seven-zero."

Brit pushed the thruster lever forward slowly. The engine purr grew to a loud roar. Water behind the craft was blown into a rooster tail by the hot gases. The boat lunged forward. A second burst of acceleration occurred as the craft rose out of the water onto the hydrofoils, greatly reducing the boat's drag coefficient. All communication between the crew members would be through their microphones and headsets. Noise aboard the gunship would approach a deadly 200 decibels.

Dempsy had contact with the enemy submarine on his scope and would be first to see incoming torpedoes. Therefore, he would control the ship's steering. Brit had the main forward thruster control. The two men must work as one. There would be no time for discussion or second guessing any orders. The first third of the battle would be to avoid the deadly "fish" for 90 seconds. During this phase of the "Game," the gunship would be fighting an exclusively defensive battle. Eston would only be a passenger. Laser blasts would not penetrate the water sufficiently to destroy charging torpedoes.

"Here they come!" yelled Dempsy.

Brit kept the ship's motion uniform. Dempsy's task would be difficult enough without accounting for speed and direc-

tional changes from the gunship as well as the incoming torpedoes. He strained to see the tell-tale wakes of foam that
would be visible just before it would be too late to maneuver
out of the way. Now he saw them off the port bow. One,
two, three ... seven; at least seven deadly wakes moving fast.

"Moving hard to port," reported Dempsy. "Give her eighty
percent throttle now!"

Brit pushed the red thruster lever away from him until the
power gauge touched eighty percent. The gunship accelerated toward the torpedoes. The velocity indicator
jumped to 180 knots. Brit could hear his seat belts strain
as they held him against the increasing g forces of acceleration. It took all of his neck muscles to keep his head steady
so he could keep a sharp eye out for other under water missiles. A large digital display on the dash in front of him tick-
ed off the seconds since entering phase I of the "Game." It
had only been 9 seconds. Brit knew the routine well.
Dempsy would head directly for the incoming torpedoes.
This maneuver served to make the gunship a smaller target, as its width was considerably less than its length. Running in the opposite direction was useless. A torpedoe's
velocity was considerably more than even this ship could
muster. Of course, heading toward the enemy torpedoes
greatly increased their relative closing speed. Dempsy and
Brit needed to react very quickly. So would the torpedoes.

Dempsy began again, "Closing time 12 seconds ... 10 ... 9 ...
8 ... turning five degrees to starboard ... 7 ... 6... 100%
thrusters now!"

Brit slammed the thruster lever as far forward as it would go. The small ship jumped again and rose so that only the very bottom surfaces of the hydrofoils were touching the water. Steering at these speeds had to be done by diverting some of the thruster gases out the small ports at the sides of the ship. They were literally flying over the water when the ominous wakes closed on them. There was no time for thought or action once the torpedoes were upon them. Closing speed was over 400 knots. Foam shot in the air around the craft. Proximity fuses on the torpedoes made them deadly even without direct contact. The gunship shot past the explosions unharmed.

Dempsy knew their craft had maintained this course too long and turned again as soon as the torpedoes had passed. There would be more on the way. They had won only a momentary victory. "Turning to two-nine-five," he advised. Then he saw it. "Torpedo from astern!" Either one of the previous seven was a smart fish or the Intruders fired one or more at 90 degrees to their present course and brought them around. "Impact in 20 seconds."

Brit knew his ship could not maintain 100 percent power for long, but didn't dare decelerate now. He could feel Dempsy trying to out maneuver the torpedo chasing them. Eston was also being thrown from side to side, the laser cannon swiveling madly with every new turn. It was all she could do to stay with the big gun.

"More fish ahead!" Dempsy warned.

Brit's mind raced, "Dempsy, are the torpedoes guided by heat, sound, or what?"

"No one really knows," returned the busy copilot.

Brit needed to make a command decision now. "I'm betting they're tracking our engines. I'll give you two seconds to turn us hard to port before I kill the main thrusters!" He counted out loud, "One and two." Dempsy didn't question the captain's orders. Just before the boat settled into the water he fired a short burst from the forward steering jets. Torpedoes screamed toward their target from both sides of the gunship.

"Now or never!" yelled Dempsy.

Brit slammed the thruster lever forward again. The engines coughed once, then came alive. The small gunboat leaped forward out of control. All three crew members strained with every muscle. Support straps pulled hard. Brit felt something snap in his lower left leg. An excruciating pain told him he had broken a bone. Had he fooled the enemy torpedoes into chasing each other? Foam wakes shot by just behind the accelerating gunship. An underwater blast shot thousands of gallons of sea into the air too close to the small craft. The shock wave hit broadside and the gunship began to careen wildly.

"We're going over!" screamed Brit. The ship rolled to 30 degrees to port.

"Noooo!" Eston was fighting with everything she had to turn the laser cannon to the port side. Her face grimaced uncontrollably as she used all the strength in her body to force the large weapon over. Pulling one foot from its stirrup she placed it against the side of the ship to help her pivot.

"Eston! The laser can't help us now. Secure yourself for the roll." commanded Brit. But, in a flash he understood. If Eston could fire the cannon high to the port side ...

Eston made position just as the gunship began to roll over. She pressed both triggers hard and held them down. The force of the impending roll pinned her to the rear of the big gun while the recoil from the repeated firing slammed the weapon into her chest. Eston hung on crying out from the exertion and the pain "Ayyyyyyyeeeeee".

Eston had done it! The recoil from the laser fire had placed sufficient force against the roll that the ship had righted and slid sideways through the water on the hydrofoils long enough for Dempsy and Brit to regain control. The digital timer on Brit's display showed 90 seconds. Phase I of the "Game" was over.

CHAPTER 4

Brit pulled back on the thruster lever until the power gauge read 30 percent. He spun and looked back at his ship and crew. The boat was apparently unharmed. Dempsy leaned back from the dash. There was blood on his right temple and Brit could tell from the way he held his mouth that his jaw was broken. "Are you O.K., Dempsy?" Dempsy nodded yes. Brit guessed that his second in command would be unable to communicate verbally for the rest of his mission. Brit looked at Eston. She was badly hurt. A small trickle of blood ran from the side of her mouth and her eyes looked glazed. Brit guessed that broken ribs had been driven through her lungs. Phase II of the "Game" would begin soon and without the gunner they would not survive. "Eston, you were wonderful. Can you hang on for phase II?"

"I think so," she whispered while trying to give a double thumbs up sign. Brit noticed her wince and saw that the thumb on her left hand was dislocated, laying back against the wrist. Eston examined her hand. "It's a good thing I'm right handed."

The team was in serious trouble. Their chances of winning this battle were not good from the start. "Phase II begins in 30 seconds," called the young captain.

Despite his special goggles Brit squinted in the bright glare while turning 360 degrees to scan the horizon. Soon the enemy ship would surface. Dempsy was again first to find the enemy vessel. Unable to speak, he moved away from his instruments long enough to point out the enemy vessel's bearing.

Brit whirled around to face the enemy ship. Eston mustered up strength from somewhere and took her position behind the laser cannon. They waited. The digital timer on Brit's dash flashed back to zero then began counting forward again. Phase II had begun. Small black dots silhouetted against the red-brown sky rose gracefully from the enemy ship and headed toward the human targets.

"Let's go," Brit said quietly to no one in particular. He pushed the thruster lever to 70 percent. Dempsy turned the boat toward the giant sun. It would be most advantageous for Eston if they could keep the missiles from coming in out of the blinding red sunlight. The crew must work as a team trying to elude or shoot down the guided missiles headed their way.

Eston flipped a small switch at the base of the laser. The sighting screen lit up. A soft steady beeping indicated there were no targets in range. She pivoted the laser toward the advancing shells. The tone and interval of beeping increased in frequency. Small bright stars materialized on the sighting screen. Each indicating an approaching missile. "Try to keep the ship on an even keel if possible," she requested "I will begin fire ... now!"

The laser barked repetitiously as Eston swung the cannon to and fro following the darting targets. The recoil of the weapon rocked the small ship making each subsequent shot more difficult. Small suns flashed in the sky overhead.

Whenever Eston scored a hit the flash would be accompanied by a great fireball. The gunship would not survive even a single missile impact. Eston was really enjoying her work. Brit and Dempsy could hear her verbal patter as she moved like a cat beneath the gun.

"Gotcha! Take that ... and that! Oh no you don't ..." The great laser had become an extension of her body. Her earlier injuries forgotten, despite their severity, Eston was lost in the action overhead. Brit was impressed. She was even better than he had heard.

Dempsy's head was buried in the dash before him. No longer able to speak, he fired the steering jets as needed for evasive action leaving Brit to read his intentions and use the thrusters as needed. The two men's special relationship was paying off. Brit saw the incoming missile in his peripheral vision just in time. He slid the thruster bar fully forward just as Dempsy fired the rear starboard jets. All three crew members were tossed to the right of the small craft, but the dodge had worked. The enemy rocket crashed harmlessly into the sea 100 yards off the starboard bow.

Eston's sighting screen was covered with tiny novas; the beeping had become a high pitched scream as the audio circuits were overloaded by the number of targets. Eston herself had stopped thinking long ago. She was totally committed to action. Her right thumb was rarely off the trigger. She dodged left, then right; high then low. Her eyes were locked on the magic screen. One target on her sight extinguished with each fireball in the sky.

Was Brit imagining it or was the beeping from Eston sight decreasing in frequency? He searched the skies trying to count the number of incoming missiles. There were only a few left! Brit couldn't believe it. They had already gotten further into the "Game" than any previous crew and it looked like they might move into Phase III. Dempsy's frantic hand waving brought him back to reality, but nearly too late. Eston, concentrating on the last of the high altitude rockets, did not seen the ringer racing in only inches off the surface of the water. She fired another short burst and the last of the high altitude missiles disintegrated. At the last second Eston saw the small star appear on her screen in the lower right hand corner. Still concentrating on the sighting screen, she swung the laser around and leveled it at the new target. Brit saw the gun pirouette and point straight at him. Eston's thumb moved for the trigger. Either she didn't real-ize the captain stood between her and the low level target or she knew that she must fire anyway. Brit didn't know which. He felt he was moving in slow motion as his mind raced. He must release his support straps and hit the deck in one smooth motion or absorb the full impact of the laser cannon only a few feet astern. He remembered childhood nightmares where he moved as if caught in molasses while trying to run from some terrible monster. The straps came loose. Brit dove for the deck and screamed simultaneously. "Shoot! Shoot!" He felt the blast of the cannon on his neck and face. The last missile exploded just off the water only a few hundred feet way.

CHAPTER 5

Brit stood quickly. A patch of uniform on his shoulder was smoldering. "We are in Phase III!" he shouted. "We need to be at the shelter in 20 seconds!" As he spoke the crew saw a single large shell leave the enemy ship and streak straight up. The small nuclear device would hover at 5000 feet for a short time, then detonate. Brit could just make out the mile long shelter floating in the distance. Any surface craft not inside the protective structure at detonation would be vaporized. Both ships would now head at top speed for the goal. When the first boat entered the shelter, solenoids would close both ends of the structure dooming the other craft.

"Dempsy this is your time to shine." Brit looked over to his combat partner, "Are you ready?"

Dempsy looked strained. As he leaned back Brit spotted the tear in his uniform over the abdomen. Dempsy was bleeding badly. Shrapnel from the last missile must have penetrated the copilots console and passed through to his body. Both men knew there were no alternatives during this battle but to continue. Brit could not take over Eston or Dempsy's capacity, nor could they take his. Dempsy's slow nod indicated he would continue as best he could. Brit turned to his station and pushed the thruster lever all the way forward. The engines screamed to life and the ship headed for the shelter at full speed. Dempsy's job would be to fire the steering rockets as efficiently as possible. The craft must take the shortest route to the shelter and cover that distance ahead of the enemy craft ... and the clock.

Brit and Eston were just passengers for now. They leaned into the acceleration eyes glued on the small enemy craft. It was impossible to tell who was ahead. Brit knew this would be a close race. He watched the timing display on his console count upward toward 20 seconds. He was worried about Dempsy and Eston. Both were seriously injured. Even on the slight chance they cleared the protective cover of the shelter before the thermonuclear device detonated, he wasn't sure either of them would live long enough to return to the training center. Brit cleared his mind. Concern for the welfare of his shipmates would not help them now. He did not like time to think during battle; a wandering mind could get them all killed. Brit concentrated on the thruster lever in his right hand.

The two ships were approaching the mile long shelter from opposite sides. Both must begin the dangerous high speed turn necessary to enter opposite sides of the floating tunnel. The terrible wrenching g forces told Brit that Dempsy was still conscious and had begun the turn. Dempsy looked up from his dash and gave a slow sober side to side nod to Brit. They weren't going to make the shelter before the enemy ship. Eston saw the negative sign as well. They would either be vaporized by the nuclear blast before entering the shelter or, with the enemy ship entering the opposite side of the shelter first triggering the entrance to close, would impact the sealed entrance to the floating tunnel at 280 knots. Either way it seemed the valiant crew of the small gunship was going to loose both the "Game" and their lives.

Eston swivelled the laser cannon to the stern. Brit knew what she was going to do, but didn't think the extra thrust would give them the edge. Nevertheless, why not go out with the gunship at full power and the laser cannon firing? Eston once again put her right thumb on the trigger and held it down. Small suns bounced off the water thousands of yards behind them. The laser recoil increased their forward velocity only slightly. Brit alternately watched his timer and the approaching shelter entrance. He read off the clock to the others, "13 ... 14 ... 15 ... It's going to be really close!" He couldn't see the enemy ship now. It would be racing directly at them trying to enter the shelter at the opposite end. "17 ... 18 ... We aren't going to make it!" The sky flashed brilliantly white temporarily blinding Brit just as the nose of their gunship entered the shelter. The blast front hit before the small ship was fully inside. Brit was thrown hard against his support straps. His hand jerked away from the thruster lever. He heard shrapnel from the gigantic blast pelting the rear of his ship. Some ricocheted past his head. He strained for the thruster control. They had made safety, but would die anyway if they hit the interior walls at full speed. He reached the lever, but his hand slipped off. In the dim interior light he could see why. His lever was covered with blood. He didn't need to turn around to know whose blood it was. Eston had still been outside of the shelter when the nuclear blast front had hit the gunship. Brit swallowed hard and reached again for the thruster control. This time he had a firm grip and began pulling back just as he saw the other ship. Miraculously, both ships must have entered the shelter simultaneously before the other entrance could be sealed.

Brit turned and looked back. Eston was gone. Her laser cannon, now twisted metal, still smoldered. Dempsy's arms swung at his sides. He was dead or at best unconscious. Brit turned back and faced the enemy ship. He returned the thruster lever to full power. They could still win the "Game" if he could ram the approaching enemy craft head on. Brit watched as the two craft screamed toward each other. The enemy ship began to turn aside, but Brit knew it was too late. Earth would win the first victory. At the last moment he screamed in anger and triumph "Dieeee!"

CHAPTER 6

Brit's fingers gripped the rails at either side of the thick padded chair. His legs struggled against the restraints on his ankles.

"Heart rate too fast! He thinks he's dying! Get him out of there now!" yelled the Game Director.

Two men in military dress pulled Brit back from the "Game" console. Each ripped a gel coated brain-link pad from the boat captain's temples.

Brit was only semi-conscious. He was aware of someone breathing hard, rasping for air. It was him. His muscles jerked spasmodically and he yelped in pain grabbing his left leg.

"Broken," one of the technicians said. "You fractured the bones straining against the restraints during the Game."

Brit looked up at the man. What was he talking about. "Dempsy? Eston? Dead?"

"He is still coming out of the link," whispered a medic to the military personnel around him. "Give him a few moments to get his bearings."

Brit looked blankly about him. He was in a large room filled with electronics. High on one wall a sign read,

BATTLE SIMULATION ROOM

and a scoreboard reported the results of past "Games".

EARTH	0	**DEATHS**	1538
INTRUDERS	0	**DEATHS**	1279

Slowly reality replaced the last remnants of electronically induced visions and Brit remembered who and where he was. The deadly "Game" with the Intruders was just that. The two races were locked in combat only through the magic of electronics. He looked over to where his friend, Dempsy, had been sitting. Medics were helping him from his chair. He looked bad. Although the battle only truly occurred inside the electronics of the sophisticated video game, the "player's" minds were fully involved. Medical science had shown centuries earlier that mental stress - translated to heart disease, ulcers and even cancer - was the most common cause of early death. As the scoreboard indicated, electronically induced deaths were common. His friend had come close.

Brit's eyes jumped to the third seat around the main "Game" console. The chair was already empty. He looked around the room just in time to see two medics push a gurney through a side door. The sheet was pulled up over the occupant's head. The gurney bumped the door jam and a woman's arm fell limp from under the cover. Eston's death during the "Game" was only electronic imagery. Now, however, it was real. He saw the scoreboard change to indicate the new status,

EARTH	0	DEATHS	1539
INTRUDERS	0	DEATHS	1282

Suddenly, all the personel in the room began chanting at once, "We won! We won!" Brit looked again at the all important scoreboard.

EARTH	1	DEATHS	1539
INTRUDERS	0	DEATHS	1282

So, they had finally won a "Game". Brit tried to be happy. It didn't work. The warriors who fought the battles were rarely as excited about winning as those on the sidelines. Visions of Eston's courageous efforts filtered out any sense of joy. Earth's first victory was hers and hers alone. He hoped she knew she had won the first in the best 2-out-of-3..

CHAPTER 7

Danny walked briskly out of the training center. The giant red sun was just rising over the blue green sea before him. A thick gloved hand moved to shade his eyes. He was already beginning to perspire in the moist heat of Vepl 7. His hand moved to adjust the black composite battle helmet to a more favorable position. The temple guards chafed, but the protective gear might save his life later. The heavy tight-fitting military dress was just as necessary and just as uncomfortable. Concentrating on the scenery again, Danny thought how odd it was that so many wars were fought in the most beautiful parts of the universe. Even in Earth's distant past, the most luxurious parts of the planet had often been selected for destruction, as if man's hatred for life extended to the Earth itself.

The Intruders had arrived ...

the end

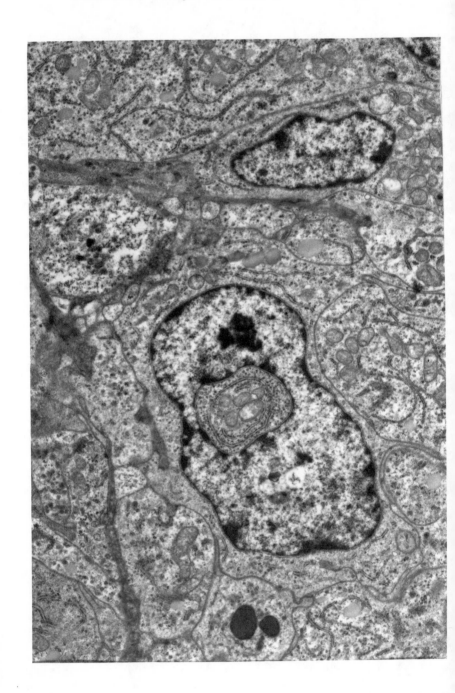

STRANGER

IN

TOWN

CHAPTER I

DAY 1: August 27th, 2 PM ...

Jeffy wandered along the road's edge looking down at his shoes, scuffing up the dust as he walked. He recalled walking this same stretch of secluded road many times before with Tracy. His older sister, by two years, had always been a real tomboy, and Jeffy loved her dearly. They had some of their best dust-bomb fights just here. Jeffy had been forced to play without his sister more and more during the last two years of her illness. Tracy had leukemia. She nearly lived at the Medical Center these days, and therefore, so did their parents. Jeffy had cried a lot. He didn't cry much anymore. He had begged God to save his sister for him and his parents. He didn't pray much anymore either. God had disappointed Jeffy.

He had grown bored with throwing small rocks at the pigs to see them squeal and run momentarily, only to loose themselves again in the all important task of eating. The dark haired, tanned youth had decided to walk to the pasture located about a half mile down the empty farm road and see if Big Red wanted to run him around for a while. The beautiful red horse always seemed anxious to see his eleven year old friend. That was more than Jeffy could say for some grownups. Well, in all fairness he thought, Grandma and Grandpa were typical doting grandparents, who indulged him too much, but they were busy today too and had told Jeffy he would have to play by himself for the rest of the afternoon.

The sun was still high and the day sparkling bright. Barn swallows swooshed down close to the fields to catch insects. Jeffy could hear grasshoppers jumping among dry volunteer grasses at the side of the road. He looked down at a particularly large green-brown beauty that had caught his attention by jumping directly across his path. Lost in admiration for the athletic insect, Jeffy didn't hear the fast moving car approaching him from behind. As his gaze rose again he was startled by the figure of a man just across the road in Baker's field. He was tall and thin and wore an unusual, one-piece, light brown jumpsuit that was nearly perfect concealment among the drying grasses. Jeffy would certainly not have detected his presence except that the camouflaged stranger had lifted a black and gray instrument to his eye, and the motion had given away his presence. Jeffy could swear the instrument was actually sitting against the man's unblinking left eye. The visitor was so absorbed in what he was doing he hadn't yet become aware of the young onlooker. Curious to see what the man saw through his special tool, Jeffy began to cross the street oblivious to the speeding pickup truck bearing down on him.

Acemk pulled the transom from his eye just in time to see the young earth child step in front of the charging machine. Acting instinctively, without considering the strict non-intervention covenant, he lunged at the endangered youngster.

Jeffy's eyes widened in fright and he threw up his arms in a defensive reflex just as the stone hard hands reached him and tossed him harshly off the road. While the boy was still in the air the man turned and faced the onrushing vehicle. Jeffy heard the loud scraping sound of tires unable to break on the loose dirt road. The next split second was reduced to slow motion in the terrified youth's mind. The front end of the pickup hit the tall figure head on. The man collapsed forward and slammed down on the hood of the pickup face first, crushing the shiny metal. The continued forward motion of the truck threw him off the hood, high in the air. He crumpled to the ground some thirty feet in front of the careening truck. Jeffy hit the ground at the same time and gasped in pain as he rolled several times and landed in the nearby field.

The truck stopped at an angle in the road. The passenger screamed, "You've killed him! Let's get out of here!"

The frightened driver made a bad decision and Jeffy heard the tires spin gravel and dirt as the vehicle fishtailed and accelerated away from the scene.

The youngster knelt, gasping and holding his ribs with both arms. He was still shaking from the shock of witnessing the terrible accident. He knew if the stranger hadn't moved as fast as he had, it would be him lying on the far side of the road. Cautiously he rose and walked over to the fallen man. "Mister, mister, are you hurt bad?" The injured man, facing away from Jeffy, didn't respond. The frightened boy moved around so he could see the man's face, "Mister, can you talk to me? Say something!" At the sight of blood issuing from multiple facial lacerations, Jeffy jumped back, "Oh, no! Oh, no!" He started to run away. Then regaining some composure, he turned back, stooped and gently reached for the fallen man's wrist to feel for a pulse. He had gained considerable hospital experience these last two years while visiting Tracy. Jeffy's fingers felt a cold hard band rather than the soft warm flesh he expected. The wrist was encircled by some kind of fancy bracelet with tiny winking lights. He dropped the man's hand. His gaze moved to the man's chest. Watching closely he could just see the chest rise and slowly fall with each breath. So, he was alive! As the boy rose to run and get help for the stranger, he spotted the gray and black tool in the road. Without thinking he picked it up and then ran down the road toward his grandparent's farmhouse. Still clutching the strange tool in his hand, he began yelling and waving as soon as the house was in sight.

Jeffy's grandparents met him at the door. "What is all the yelling about?"

"A man ... a man was hit by a red truck," wheezed Jeffy gasping for breath from his long run. "And then they just drove off! He saved my life Grandma!"

Grandma grabbed him by the shoulders and looked directly into the boy's eyes. "Was he killed, honey?" Then, realizing an 11 year old probably wouldn't know, she added, "Can he speak or move?"

"No. He's hurt really bad, grandma."

"Grandma, you call the police. Jeffy and I will go see if we can be any help," said Grandpa. Jeffy dropped the device he had carried back from the accident on the kitchen table as he and Grandpa ran out the door.

CHAPTER 2

August 27th, 2:23 PM ...

Hank was leaning against the nurse's station just outside emergency when the call came over the police radio. "Unit 3. Hit and run victim three miles south on Mellon Road at Baker's field." A short pause was followed by, "Hey, Hank, this is Bill. Are you listening to me?"

Hank reached back behind the desk and fingered the mike, "O.K., O.K., I'm on my way." "Bill was a good cop and a close friend, but too anxious in tight situations," Hank thought. And his driving! Bill loved fast cars and had considerable experience at 'flying low'! The ER nurse jogged down the hall to the exit door where his ambulance was parked, slowing only long enough to call down a side hallway to a young doctor, "Hop to it, Dave, we've got a code 4 run." Dave dropped the journal he had been reading and ran toward the exit. He hated car accidents, but loved emergency room duty, and the extra money it earned him. He hadn't yet shut the door on his side of the ambulance when the lights and siren came on and Hank pulled away.

In less than three minutes Hank pulled his ambulance up to the knot of police and civilians on the dirt road. They were both out of the vehicle before the sound of the siren had died. Rushing to the injured man's side, Dave felt the neck for a pulse and found a reassuring slow throb. "He's got a steady pulse, Hank. Will you examine his extremities for any serious bone breaks or bleeding? I'll try to determine the extent of internal injuries before we move him." Dave pulled on the man's tunic so he could put the stethoscope on his chest. The tunic didn't give. He looked for buttons or a zipper. Finding none he slid the silver cup down the tunic neck and placed in over the heart.

"He is bleeding from lacerations on both thighs, Dave, but I can't get a good look. I don't feel any broken bones. This guy's outfit must be made of steel. I can't cut or tear it," said Hank.

"Yeh. I know. I'm having the same trouble." Dave opened a plastic bottle of sterile saline and carefully washed the blood and dust from the victim's face and eyes. Pulling a small penlight from his shirt pocket, he moved so that his body shaded the injured man's face. Gently he held one eyelid, then the other, open while he passed the small beam of light across each pupil. Something still clouded the eyes. "I can't visualize the pupils well, Hank, but I think they are reacting to light. He's got brain function. Let's get him to the hospital."

CHAPTER 3

August 27th, 2:33 PM ...

With the ambulance's arrival at the emergency entrance of the medical center, the staff began the now routine trauma care activities that they had rehearsed to perfection. Every doctor and nurse knew exactly what to do. The patient's gurney was quickly rolled to a far wall in the emergency room and he was deftly transferred to a mobile bed. A small mask that just covered the nose and mouth was placed over the man's head. Someone's hand reached to one of the many stainless steel gas outlet valves on the wall and oxygen enriched, breathing air bubbled up through a small container of water to a clear plastic tube connected to the face mask. Only Dave's concise unemotional directions to the various team members broke the soft sounds of sterile paper wrappers being opened, surgical rubber gloves snapping and the tear of the velcro band on a blood pressure cuff.

"Let's get this uniform, or whatever it is, off him now," commanded Dave. "This guy was hit hard. I expect broken bones and significant soft tissue damage," he continued while trying to find a zipper or some fastening device on the tunic. His fingers found a small gap at the neck of the tan uniform and he pulled. The material parted soundlessly down an invisible seam that stretched to the waist and then continued down the left leg. With the tunic removed, the staff got their first good look at the injured man. The team examined the patient before them wordlessly.

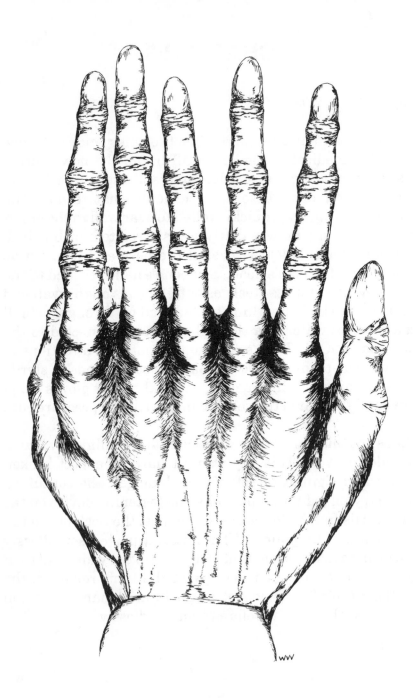

Hank broke the silence, "What do you make of this, Dave, multiple system birth defects or what?"

The man before them had seven digits on each hand and foot, each digit with four, no five Dave counted, joints. There were no fingernails or toenails. He had two umbilici and the full rib cage guarded an enlarged chest cavity.

Someone whistled and then commented, "Look at that, two inees. I've seen guys with no belly button after laparotomy, but I've never seen anyone with extras."

"Shake it loose. We need to proceed if we are going to save this patient," snapped Dave trying to show less surprise than he really felt. "I'm going to finish cleaning off the face and eyes. Pete, you draw blood for routine chemistries, complete blood count and type and cross. Our man looks off color to me. He may have problems not directly related to the accident."

Pete turned one arm with the oversized hand palm up and felt the skin for a rubber-like rebound that would indicate a blood vessel close to the surface. "Odd," he reported to no one in particular. "I can't find the antecubital veins. Ah, here's something. Well, they aren't where they are suppose to be, but he does have veins." Pete wrapped a rubber tube around the upper arm to trap the venous blood in the extremity and disinfected the spot over the target vein with alcohol. As he inserted the needle, blood rushed back into the syringe. "This guy's blood looks a little thin, Dave, I'll ask for a hematocrit as well."

"Good idea, Pete. Internal bleeding wouldn't surprise me. What I can't understand is why there aren't broken bones." Dave pulled the ophthalmoscope off the wall and holding it close to his right eye focused the lens on the palm of his hand. When he was satisfied it was set correctly, he bent down to examine the comatose patient's eyes. As the light from the instrument fell on the first eye, the shorter wavelengths were reflected back casting blue designs on Dave's face. The examining physician strained to see the star-like vascular pattern that would tell him he was looking at the retina in the back of the eye. "Something is still clouding the retina, I can't make out the ... what!" Dave jumped back involuntarily, dropping the ophthalmoscope. The delicate instrument, arced down on the power cord and slammed against the wall. Pieces of glass and metal shot out onto the floor. Everyone jumped.

"What is it, Dave?" asked Hank, moving to help his ashen friend.

"Something is wrong. We need a history on this patient and we need it now! Betty," Dave called out to the desk secretary, "tell hospital security that I want to see them, pronto." Dave continued, still clearly unnerved by what he had just seen, "Someone else better check this man's eyes. Unless I am hallucinating, there are LED's and liquid crystal digits in front of the retina."

"That's not all, Dave," reported Hank in a sober tone, "There's a bracelet on his left wrist. I know it's impossible, but even though it contains electronics of some sort it seems to be literally growing from his wrist! I'd swear it is really part of his anatomy! Also, I can see muscle tissue through the laceration on his left thigh. The tissue has alternating green and yellow banding." Hank's eyes met Dave's. "He is human, isn't he Dave? Dave?"

Dave stared at Hank for a full 15 seconds before turning without responding to his friends query. "We have just about done all we can here. I want this man admitted as John Doe and moved to an isolation room on 5 North. No one, repeat NO ONE, divulges anything that has happened here. Hank, you are this man's nurse. Don't leave his side. Get a tissue sample for cytology before you sew up that leg. Leave the I.V. in. If his condition changes, beep me. I need to make a call."

After the lead physician's departure, the trauma staff hesitated momentarily. Hank took charge. "O.K. people let's finish up and move him out like the good doctor Smith said."

CHAPTER 4

August 27th, 4:53 PM ...

Charging into his office, Dave hesitated at his secretary's desk only long enough to request a little too sternly, "Get hold of Dr. Phlag and have him meet me in my office. Then call the sheriff's office and have Bill get hold of me. Then, look up Henry Catlen's number at the Center for Disease Control's Special Cases section and place the call for me. Transfer the calls to my office when you get either of them on the line."

"I'm fine and how are you today?" Dora called after him as he closed the door to the inner office.

Dave stood at his desk staring out the office window. He was so lost in thought that he jumped when the first call came through.

"Hi, Dave. This is Bill. Before you ask, there is nothing else to report on your motor vehicle accident victim. I couldn't even find footprints in the field to help pinpoint where the man had been coming from when little Jeffy saw him ..."

"Quiet Bill and listen!" Dave interrupted. "You must trust me on this. I want you to put up a roadblock around the accident site. Nobody should be allowed near there. And Bill, I want you to stop traipsing around the field too."

"Now wait a minute, Dave. We are friends and all, but I am the law around here and I will make those kinds of decisions," retorted Bill somewhat offended.

"Sorry Bill, I did come off too strong. Please take my word on this. When you have the roadblock up come in to the hospital and I will tell you what this is all about. I really don't want to say any more over the phone right now."

"O.K. ... O.K. I guess a roadblock to prevent losing any physical evidence concerning the hit and run is reasonable, but I want an explanation when I get in there."

"You'll get it. Thanks, Bill." Dave hung up the phone.

Dora's sulking voice came over the intercom as the chief of pathology walked into the office, "Dr. Phlag is here and Henry Catlen is on line 2."

"Hi Lawrence," Dave said without looking up, "Have a seat while I take this call. You should hear this anyway."

Dave picked up the receiver and punched the blinking button. "Henry, I think we need help out here."

"Dave old man! Must be ten years since we interned together at that museum of a hospital in Chicago. I see your manners haven't improved any. Aren't you suppose to say 'hello' or 'how are you and the misses' or something?" Henry responded jovially.

"I'm sorry, Henry, this really isn't the time. I have our pathologist here with me and I am going to put you on the intercom system so he can join us in this if that is O.K.?" Dave was all business.

"What is this about, Dave?" the pathologist's curiosity was peeked now.

"I'd rather we just do this once, Lawrence," Dave said holding up an index finger. He set the phone handset down on the special intercom box and fingered the switch. Sitting down and leaning forward on his desk, he motioned Lawrence to move his chair closer in. "Can you still hear me, Henry?"

"Loud and clear." Henry's voice came over the intercom.

Dave began explaining the events of the day in chronological order. As soon as he began detailing the anatomical abnormalities of the stranger, Henry interrupted. "Tell me this isn't a joke, Dave."

"I almost wish it were," he answered.

"Just a moment." Lawrence and Dave heard Henry set the phone down. A few moments later Henry was back on the line. "Bear with me a minute, Dave. I want to be sure this line is clear." A small beep was followed by a new voice on the line.

"Communications Security. What do you need, Colonel?" came an all too military sounding voice.

"We need a class one quiet-line here, Captain. Can you take care of that now?" Henry's voice responded.

Lawrence looked at Dave and raised his eyebrows.

"This is all news to me," whispered Dave.

"No problem, Colonel. Give us 30 seconds," came the reply.

Soft beeps, buzzes and whistles issued from the intercom. Then the line seemed to clear. "That should do it, Colonel. This is Captain Lewis, five-five-two, indexing and signing over to Colonel Henry Catlen." The military voice apparently disconnected.

"What was that all about, Henry?" asked Dave, "And since when is it Colonel?"

"Never mind that now. Continue with your story."

Lawrence was leaning on the desk in rapped attention. Dave completed describing the new patient. Finally, he told them which lab tests he had ordered so far.

Henry directed his first comments to Dr. Phlag. "Lawrence, do you have Class III biological hazard hoods in the lab, electron microscopy facilities and a cell culture unit?"

"That's an affirmative times three," the pathologist answered.

"Simple yes's and no's would be good right now," Henry chastised the pathologist for his sarcastic attempt at military prose. "I will fly out as soon as possible. Meanwhile, you must follow my next directions exactly! Understood Dave?"

"What's happening here, Henry? I phoned for advice not military intervention," replied Dave.

"Perhaps it hasn't yet occurred to you Dave, but the most dangerous threat the earth has ever known may be in your hospital right now. If that man, or whatever he is, isn't from earth, he poses a terrible biological threat to the human race. Normal bacterial and viral flora, not to mention any active infectious process he may be suffering from, will be totally alien to our immune system. Remember Plague, a disease natural to this planet, wiped out one fourth of the population of Europe in the 14th century. Imagine what a disease new to this planet could do? Your first responsibility is to quarantine that patient and prevent any more contact by hospital personnel than is absolutely necessary. Use only those staff members who have already been exposed when someone must have contact with him. Frankly I think we are too late to be sure we can contain any problems. I'm going to order the town closed by the National Guard immediately."

Things were moving too fast for Dave. "Henry! Do you really think that is necessary?"

"Haven't you been listening to me, Dave? Do you have any idea what possibilities must be entertained in the event an infectious agent is isolated from the stranger? I'm being conservative in my actions right now. Things may get much worse. Calling us was the right thing to do. Dr. Phlag, you are still there?"

"Yes, I'm here." The pathologist was dead serious now.

"I want you to work up all tissues and fluids obtained from the new patient under a Class III hood. Assign a volunteer technologist to handle the specimens. Anyone who has already worked with them has volunteered, by the way. Run every test at your disposal to determine if the man is suffering from any microbial diseases."

"How would I know if he were," asked the pathologist.

"You're the pathologist. Presume that tissue damage or inflammation associated with any organism reflects disease. We are obviously working at a disadvantage here," acknowledged Henry. "Dave?"

"Yeh, Henry"

"I'm flying out as soon as possible. Can you take care of things until I get there?" Henry tried to speak soothingly now.

"I guess so, Henry. Henry ... this could all just be a mistake. Right?" Dave offered hopefully.

"I don't think so, Dave, and neither do you. See you in 48 hours."

Lawrence was quiet for a moment. "Well," he began medita-
tively, "I better get started. Some of the specimens are already in the lab then?"

"Yes. If you need anything else I left Hank in charge of the
patient. He and the rest of the trauma team, as well as
myself have already been exposed. So have Bill and the boy
and his grandparents. Henry's right. We may have already
lost control of a potentially epidemic situation," admitted
Dave.

"We can't change what has already happened," Lawrence
consoled, "but we can be careful from here on out. I will call
you before I leave the hospital." The pathologist stopped at
the door. "On second thought, we better all sleep here for a
few days. No sense exposing anyone else."

Dave moved over to the window and stared out at the small
town. He hoped the lab specimens would be negative.

CHAPTER 5

DAY 2: August 28th, 7:12 AM ...

Dave got off the elevator at the 5th floor. His surgical greens looked like he had slept in them. A security guard stood outside a room at the far end of the ward. Dave headed for the room stopping first at the nurse's station to look at John Doe's chart. He pulled the metal jacketed chart from a hook labelled ROOM 561 and leaned with his back against the high counter. Instantly a terrible itch attacked the back of his throat and his eyes began to tear. Turning he saw the cause of his problem. "Nurse could you move the flowers into the office, please? I am deathly allergic to roses." Dave moved away from the desk and began reading the chart. The ward nurse returned and watched quietly as the physician concentrated on the chart in his hands.

The first tests had been completed. Bright red results on every lab slip indicated abnormal values. John Doe was anemic having only 40% of the expected red cells in his blood and, more importantly, the complete count had shown six distinct types of white cells - all unidentifiable. His blood sugar was low and his electrolytes were all wrong. "Oh, my word!" escaped his lips as he read the cytology report. Rather than the expected 23 pair of chromosomes, the strange patient in room 561 had 27 pair. There was no doubt any longer. John Doe was not human!

"Dr. Smith I have some questions," the nurse began.

"Sorry, I can't answer anything right now." He looked at her for a moment. She knew these results and knew what they meant. "I will tell you everything as soon as possible," he added. Returning the chart to its hanger, Dave headed toward the guarded room.

A large warning sign had been hung below the room number on the door.

CLASS III BIOHAZARD AREA

ABSOLUTELY NO ADMITTANCE

WITHOUT PERMISSION

"So, am I allowed in there?" Dave asked the guard.

"Of course, Dr. Smith, I was told to expect you. But, you will have to gown, glove and put on a mask," said the big man pointing to a special cart sitting at the end of the hall.

"Yes, I understand," acknowledged Dave.

Gowned and gloved, Dave stepped into the room and was met by an astounding sight. John Doe, still apparently unconscious, had been raised to a nearly sitting position. Playing over one eye was the bright beam of an opthamologist's slit lamp. The apparatus sent a thin beam of light onto the patient's eye while the doctor looked through a complicated lens system which allowed him to visualize any scratches or injuries on the eye's surface. What was startling was the spectacular display of blue light that bounced around the room as the slit lamp was adjusted.

The opthamologist looked up. "Interesting, huh Dave? This guy's eyeballs are covered with some type of dichroic material. When a bright light is shown on his cornea the dangerous blue wavelengths are reflected away and only a subdued yellow-red light is allowed to enter the eye. His color vision, if he has color vision, would certainly be affected, however, I would guess this man could look directly at the sun with no ill effects."

"He isn't a man you know," replied Dave quite seriously.

"Yeh, I know," countered the opthamologist.

Dave saw Hank sitting in a large chair at the side of the room. "He looked tired. He probably slept the night with John Doe," thought Dave. Right now all Hank needed to do was stay out of the other medical staff's way. Clearly that was all right with him.

Dr. Phlag was in the room too. "I take it you have looked at the patient's chart, Dave?"

"Yes," was his only reply. He looked at the patient for some time while the opthamologist adjusted the color of light on the slit-lamp in an attempt to get a better look into the eye or at least gain some understanding of the dichroic film covering it. Dave eventually moved to examine his patient before leaving the room. "When will the first electron microscopy pictures be available, Lawrence?" he asked.

"Probably not until early tomorrow. We want to be sure we don't damage the cells during fixation. I suspect these films will be hard enough to evaluate without accounting for artifacts we have introduced during processing," the pathologist answered.

"O.K. Well, I've got plenty to do. Let me know if his mental status changes, Hank."

"Uh huh," was the only response Hank gave.

Dave peeled off the gown and gloves and placed them in the receptacle beside a small sink. After washing his hands carefully three times he left the room. "Coming out," he warned the security guard.

Grandpa put on his coat and reached for the car keys on the kitchen counter. Grandma picked up the strange looking toy Jeffy had left on the table. She tried poking at some projections that looked like buttons. Nothing happened. "These new toys all look alike to me," she said to her husband. "I think the batteries are dead. Pick up some C cells at the hardware store while you are downtown, will you honey?"

"How do you know what size to get?" he asked.

"Well, I don't know. Don't they all take the C cells now? Even if they don't work in this, the children can always use more batteries," Grandma countered.

Grandpa shrugged his shoulders and left. Grandma carried the toy upstairs and set it on Jeffy's bedside table. "He will find it later," she thought, "and now I can finish cleaning house."

CHAPTER 6

DAY 3: August 29th, 8:36 AM ...

Dave entered John Doe's room. There had been no change in the patient in the last 24 hours. He was still comatose. More lab tests simply confirmed his being an alien, but hadn't yet let them know what they might do to save his life. Marie, Chief of Dental Service, was probing deep into the unconscious man's mouth. A portable dentist's drill stood beside the bed. "Hi, Dave," she greeted him. "I would love to be able to offer you the same dental protection our unusual guest has here. Some kind of plastic or resin coating protects his teeth. It gives him a somewhat pinkish opalescent grin. Had you noticed that?"

"No, can't say I really spent much time checking him for cavities," Dave answered with a smile. "So this is pretty tough stuff is it?"

"I'll say. I've tried every pick and drill bit I have. None of them are even any good anymore. You would have to use a jack hammer to get through this stuff, and in fact, I don't really think that would work either. By the way, the orthopedic people think his bones may be covered with a similar compound. John Doe here didn't even break a pinky when he was hit, yet the flesh trauma and facial injuries suggest he should have been killed."

Dave approached the bed to watch the dentist work. As he looked at John Doe's face close up he noticed something.

"This doesn't look right," he said carefully running his opened hands across the patients temples. "I think he is beginning to swell here and here," he pointed to the sides of the man's head. "Hank, call X-ray and ask them to bring up the portable unit immediately."

Marie removed her tools and rolled the drill stand away from the bed. "Guess I am finished here anyway," she commented. "I'll get out of your way for a while."

"Thanks, Marie. I will let you know what happens here. By the way, you know you won't be allowed to leave the hospital for a while now that you have had contact with our patient," Dave warned.

"Yes, I am aware of the risks, but just like everyone else, I couldn't pass up the chance to examine Johnny here," Marie answered. She gave Dave a quick smile and left the room.

Dave's beeper squealed. Then Dr. Phlag's voice announced over the small speaker, "Dave, better come to pathology now. The electron micrographs are developed."

"I'm going to be in pathology, Hank. Call me when the X-Ray people have the skull series for me."

"O.K. Dave. The X-rays should be ready within the hour."

Dave flew into the small room that contained the hospital's electron microscope. "So what do the films show, Lawrence?"

"Bad news, I'm afraid. Look at these." Dr. Phlag laid several black and white pictures on the small counter that ran the length of one wall. "I make out intra-nuclear inclusions in virtually every cell!"

"Oh, no!" was Dave's reply. "I don't suppose these are artifacts created by the fixation process?"

"Every cell in every sample is the same. The inclusions are real," Dr. Phlag confirmed.

Dave scanned the prints one by one. Sure enough, every cell had an area of dark granular material inside the nuclear membrane. "So, this guy's an alien. What would you expect his cells to look like," Dave retorted defensively. "This doesn't really prove anything does it?"

"Dave, you don't have to be a pathologist to recognize rampant viral infection. Sure, John Doe has extra chromosomal DNA, but what we are looking at here is viral inclusions and you know it. I have never seen this degree of tissue involvement. The virus must be either a very slow killer or perhaps lives synergistically with this guy without causing disease. In either case we don't know whether it is infectious for humans."

Dave's beeper went off again. "Dr. Smith, there is a Henry Catlen from the CDC waiting in your office."

"Why do you carry that thing anyway," said Lawrence, "I threw my beeper away years ago."

"Good idea," agreed Dave, "but too late now. Guess I better go tell Henry the bad news. Do we have any viral cultures set up on these specimens? I know that will be his first question."

"Sure do. I was just on my way to check with virology and see if they have any preliminary results. I'll come to your office as soon as I can. I want to meet Colonel Catlen," Lawrence called after Dave as he headed out of the stuffy room toward his office.

Dave strode into his office. "Hi, Henry, it really is good to see you. How's the family?"

"Too late to ask that now, you already muffed it on the phone the other day," Henry responded smiling and taking his friend's hand. "However, I'm fine and not married. Thanks for asking. So, enough of this. How is your patient? I want to hear everything. Don't suppose you brought his chart down with you did you? Will he live? Is he awake yet? What are the microbiology and virology results?" Henry fired question after question without waiting for an answer.

"O.K., O.K.! One thing at a time. Here sit," Dave said pointing to the chair near his desk. Dave began detailing everything that had happened since he had phoned the Colonel. He had not yet gotten to the electron microscopy results when Dora announced that Dr. Phlag was waiting. "Send him in, Dora." Dave pulled another chair up to his desk for the third man. Henry stood.

"Hello, Dr. Catlen I presume. Or is it Colonel Catlen?" Lawrence held out his hand.

"Actually it's both. Call me Henry."

"Let's hear it, Lawrence, what did virology say," Dave questioned the pathologist.

"Virology? You better fill me in," demanded the newly arrived CDC officer.

"The first series of electron micrographs indicate our new patient has a consuming viral infection," explained the pathologist. "We don't know if it is normal for him nor do we know if the agent is infective in human tissue. It's a queer thing, Dave," Lawrence continued, "the cell cultures inoculated with John Doe's specimens are still healthy, but there is some indication that they are reverting to a normal tissue state. In the case of a cell culture of course that's bad. The cells are dying, but there is no proof that a virus is directly involved. We have lost cell lines before."

"I need to know the minute there is any hard evidence that an infectious agent has been isolated from the alien," Henry stated in a serious tone. "Meanwhile I would like to see this John Doe myself." Henry rose indicating Dave and Lawrence should take him to the patient's room now.

CHAPTER 7

DAY 4: August 30th, 7:00 AM ...

Dave arrived at the isolation ward early. He wanted a chance to review John Doe's chart before Henry Catlen began asking him more questions. Besides, it was beginning to look like the strange patient's health was deteriorating. Dave sat at the nurse's station and thumbed through the chart. As he reached absently to rub his forehead something pricked the back of his hand. Dave winced and looked up. Someone had left another rose on the counter and his hand had brushed against one of the thorns. "Nurse, there is a rose out here again," he called obviously annoyed. He reached to rub the tears from his eyes out of habit before realizing that he wasn't suffering from his usual allergy attack. "That's odd," he said to no one in particular.

"Pardon me," answered the duty nurse.

"Oh, nothing. Sorry I barked at you. Normally flowers drive my allergies crazy," the doctor apologized.

Dave entered the alien's room to find Dr. Phlag carefully examining John Doe's skull. "Could be bad news, Dave," the pathologist began. "John Doe may be in trouble. You were right, or partially right, about the swelling around his head. Only it isn't really swelling, but demineralization of the cranial bones. In simple terms, the bones in his face and head are beginning to soften. Who knows if this is some unusual disease process or ..."

157

"Or what, Lawrence," Dave prompted.

"Well, what's to say this isn't the beginning of some ordinary developmental phase. Perhaps he is going through a simple period of cerebral growth or even a complete metamorphosis like some giant butterfly. We haven't a clue as to what is normal for this guy."

"Being comatose is certainly not normal," countered Dave. "I would give anything to be able to ask him some questions."

"Wouldn't we all," said the pathologist. "Oh, yes. Henry called just before you arrived. He wants us to meet him in the cafeteria."

"Might as well," Dave responded somewhat dejectedly. "We certainly aren't doing our patient any good here."

7:15 AM ... 6th floor cancer ward

Phil pushed open the door to his friend's private room on the cancer ward. "So, Dan, how are we feeling today?"

"Don't use 'we' when you talk to me Phil. I'm a doctor too, remember? In answer to your question I feel pretty good for a man with end stage leukemia. As a matter of fact I'm hungry! Can you beat that? I haven't been hungry since you started feeding me cytotoxins."

"I'm glad you are feeling better, but it is rather hard to understand. Frankly, your last blood work didn't look too promising. And, speaking of cytotoxin chemotherapy ...

Nurse, hand me the syringe please." Phil swabbed the injection port on the intravenous bottle hanging beside Dan's bed with a disinfectant wipe, waited a moment, then uncapped the syringe and injected the medication. He continued to speak while he removed the bottle from the hanger and rotated it to mix the medication. "Since this will probably kill your appetite soon we will get you something nummy to eat now. Nurse, see to getting this old grump some apple pie or something, O.K.?"

Sally smiled at her favorite employer, now patient, "So, what will it be, Dan, chocolate cream or apple?"

"Apple with ice cream will do nicely, nurse," he responded jovially.

Sally patted the spot where her emaciated friend's stomach used to be and with raised eyebrows said, "With ice cream?" After giving him one last adoring pat she left the room with Phil, taking the medication cart with her.

"He really looks good today, huh?"

"He is dying, Sally, you and I both know that."

Sally scowled at Phil and walked with him to Tracy's room without further comment. Phil had a way of always reinforcing reality when she wasn't really interested in thinking clearly.

They hesitated outside the small girl's room. Phil looked at Sally, "Sorry, Sally. He is a friend of mine too. Some mornings I hate cancer rounds and maintaining a realistic outlook allows me to function objectively." She hadn't really expected an apology and really shouldn't have needed one. They looked at each other for a moment. "O.K. time to see little Tracy," Phil said. He visibly shook his head as if to physically dislodge the sadness from his face, and briskly pushed open the door.

Tracy's mother was sitting at her bedside reading from a story book. Phil interrupted, "So, hey there kiddo, how are you feeling today?"

"I feel much better, Dr. Jones, I'm hungry. When can we take this tube out of my nose and let me eat regular stuff again?" replied Tracy.

"She has been more alert and in better spirits this morning than anytime since her admission," added Mrs. Anderson. "Would it be possible to let her try solid food?"

Phil looked at Tracy through a clinician's eyes. She did look better. "Must be something in the air today. All our patients are getting better no matter what we do," commented Phil lightly.

Sally filled a small syringe with medicine from a rubber stoppered bottle. She held the syringe up to the light checking the volume aspirated, then handed the syringe and the medicine bottle to Phil. "125 milligram dose," she spoke softly.

"We'll see about food soon. Right now we are going to begin that medicine we talked to you about yesterday. All right?". Phil began to disinfect the injection port on Tracy's I.V. without waiting for an answer.

At the ward nurses' station, two uniformed doctors reviewed charts occasionally commenting on the patient whose notes they were scrutinizing. In back of them three monitors displayed the heartbeats of seriously ill patients. The tracings on the green CRTs rose and fell leaving a pretty trail of fading waveforms matched by a soft beeping with each heartbeat. Under each of the monitors was taped the name and room number of the patient. The trail on the center monitor flickered once then became a flat line. Beneath the monitor white tape read "Dan Nichols." The soft beeping changed to a long high squeal. Both doctors turned. The one closest to the monitor pushed a test button on the unit, waited momentarily, then moved to the nurses' station and flipped a large red toggle labelled "CODE."

A soft gong rang in the hall four times. Phil glanced quickly at Sally. To any patients the quietly sounding alarm would not be noticed among the other constant PA system announcements and bells always going off in a medical center, but the staff knew this was a Code signal. Someone had died or was near death. Phil handed Sally the syringe, "You can do this. I better see if they need any help." He left the room without further comment.

"Where is Dr. Phil going?" asked Tracy.

"He will be right back, honey. Someone is sick." answered Sally. She moved to inject the medication, but her hands were shaking and she was afraid Tracy would notice. It couldn't be Dan, she thought, I haven't gotten him his pie and ice cream.

Phil charged into Dan's room. The two younger doctors and a nurse were right behind him with a crash cart. Dan was sitting up in bed. He stared unblinking at the ceiling. "Get that cart out of here!" Phil yelled at the other medical staff. "Dan didn't want heroics and under the circumstances I can't see any reason either." Phil moved to the side of his friend. "Something isn't right. He was hungry just before we gave him the medication. He looked good today," he said to the others. "Get him to pathology stat. Draw blood for chemistry now." Phil looked up, "He and Tracy were both feeling better ...." He hurdled over the bed and dashed out the door without finishing the sentence.

Phil lunged into Tracy's room already talking, "Sally, don't give the cytotoxin ..."

Sally, Tracy and Mrs. Anderson all jumped at the intrusion. Phil saw the syringe, still full, laying on the medication tray. "Sorry, guys," he said regaining his composure. "I think, nurse, that we will wait on Tracy's medication for a bit yet.

She does look good. Sally, will you come with me for a moment?"

In the hall, Phil quickly explained. "Dan is dead, Sally. It is probably for the best. He died quickly." Without giving the nurse time to mourn the loss of her friend he continued, "However, I'm concerned over the way he died. I want you to take the syringe and medication bottle to toxicology immediately. Also, I want to go back in and get oral scrapings from Tracy. I will take the specimen to the lab myself. Immediately. Understand?"

Sally nodded yes.

They re-entered Tracy's room. "We need another specimen from you honey," Sally said.

Tracy flinched. She knew what 'another specimen' could mean when you had leukemia. "Do I have to now. I really feel good!"

Sally understood. "This is going to be easy, Tracy. We are just going to swab the inside of your mouth."

"But, her mouth is so sore most of the time from virus infections," her mother offered. "Please be careful."

Sally had Tracy open her mouth and carefully scraped the inside of her cheek with a sterile tongue depressor. Tracy didn't even flinch. Sally placed the wooden stick into a sterile paper sleeve, picked up the medication tray and followed Phil from the room once again.

"No wonder Tracy feels like eating. The sores in her mouth are gone," Sally told Phil. Phil knew something he wasn't sharing. She could see it in his eyes. "What is it? Phil, what do you suspect?"

Phil took the tongue blade from her. "Not yet, Sally. I will take this specimen to the lab. Make sure Dan goes to autopsy as soon as possible. We can't save him, but he may be able to help us save Tracy. Dan would have liked that." He walked away quickly heading for pathology and lab services.

Cytology lab ...

Kathleen leaned over the microtome examining the floating sections for one just the right color. The machine slowly rocked a piece of tissue imbedded in wax across a razor sharp blade. With each pass a thin wafer of wax and tissue would be pushed onto the surface of a small vessel of water. When a section was the correct thickness it would be smooth on the water and reflect a blue opalescence. There, there was a good one now. She dipped her slide into the water, brought it up to the floating section and pulled and lifted at the same time. The microscopically thin segment stuck to the center of the glass slide and came out of the bath perfectly.

Phil came crashing in the door. "Kathleen, I need this cheek tissue stained for chromosomal patterns stat."

"Dr. Jones, everything in the laboratory is stat. You know that. Don't you ever knock or anything? I could have lost a nearly perfect section."

"Sorry. This is serious. More important I think than anything you have ever done before. Whose tissue are you working on right now?" Phil continued, breathless from his jog to the laboratory.

"Our John Doe on 5 North. More chromosomal stains and electron microscopy. What's going on with your patient?"

Phil didn't answer her question. "Electron microscopy, of course! Do that with my specimen too. I'll make out an authorization now."

"Don't tell me. Let me guess. You want me to look for any unusual intra-nuclear inclusions on electron microscopy and any extra chromosomal elements in the stained sections. Right?" said Kathleen.

"Exactly! And I want the same done on Dr. Nichol's tissue as soon as he hits the morgue," Phil replied.

Kathleen blurted, "Oh no! When did Dan die."

"I apologize again, Kathleen," Phil said softly, "I forgot you were a friend of his too. He just died a few minutes ago. Do him and all of us a favor and hop on this work. I wasn't kidding when I said there may be something really unusual going on here. If I am right we may be in serious trouble. You can beep me at 5-2634 when you find out anything. By the way, you don't happen to have a bellboy number for that doc visiting from the Center for Disease Control do you?"

"Sure do. His name is Henry Catlen and his number is 5-2400. He and Dr. Jones just dropped off the tissue samples from John Doe. They said they were headed to the cafeteria for coffee."

"Thanks again, Kathleen," Phil said as he headed out of the lab to let her work.

"I haven't had any coffee today," she called after him.

Hospital cafeteria ...

Phil found David and his friend from CDC sitting at a back table in the cafeteria. He joined them without asking. "We need to talk. Dan is dead."

"Oh, I'm sorry to hear that," said Dave. "He was a good man and a fine physician. We will miss him around here."

"The problem is Dan was feeling really good this morning and he died too soon after we gave him his latest load of cytotoxin. That isn't all," continued Phil, "my other leukemia patient, Tracy, appears to be entering a remission. Yesterday I wouldn't have given her much chance to live out the month. Today she wants solid food and looks good."

"I don't follow, Phil. What connection can you see between Dan's death and Tracy's feeling better? They just don't sound like related events to me," said Dave.

Henry was more impressed. "When I first arrived this morning, I overheard a cytology tech telling you his cell culture line had been destroyed. Isn't that right, Dave?"

"Not exactly," Dave explained. "What he said was that it was as if the malignant cell line had been 'cured' of its disease. As you know, normal human tissue cells can only be grown in culture in the lab for a few generations over a period of weeks. Then they die out. Cancer cells will continue to grow indefinitely. The malignancy changes their genetic structure and they become 'immortal' in culture. Our cell line we have been using for virus work in the lab seems to have spontaneously cured itself and then, like any healthy tissue, died out in culture. It is very odd. I have never heard of a malignant line of cells reverting to a healthy state."

Henry pressed on, "Dave I want you to tell your tech to take any cells you have left and send them to pathology for chromosomal stain and electron microscopy for nuclear inclusions."

"Oh boy," said Phil as he rose from the table.

"Where are you going?" called Dave.

"I think I better buy Kathleen some coffee," he said over his shoulder.

"Me thinks that man may need a rest," said Dave shrugging his shoulders. Henry looked frightfully stern. "You have on your Colonel face all of a sudden, Henry. What's up?"

Henry got up to go. "I'm afraid its time for me to make a call, Dave. I will meet you in the lab later."

Dave's beeper signalled and Hank's voice came from the small speaker, "Dave, you better come up to 5 North."

Colonel Catlen walked out of the hospital and headed for the phone booth on the corner. The booth door was jammed. It took considerable pulling and banging to release the warped hinges. Finally entering, he picked up the receiver and dialed zero without putting in a coin. "This is Colonel Henry Catlen," he said in a business tone to the operator. "Please connect me with 212-454-0999 collect."

A pleasant voice on the other end of the line said she would accept the charges. "This is Watchwoman," she said. "To whom do you wish to speak, please."

"Sanitation," was Henry's reply.

The voice on the other end of the line faltered. She had not expected that request.

Henry didn't wait for the coded formalities to finish. "This is Colonel Henry Catlen. Repeat, Colonel Henry Catlen. I am reporting biofire in Centerville, Washington. Code lock, one dash, two dash, niner dash, five. Require immediate closure. Prepare to sterilize in 72 hours unless otherwise notified. I stand at ground zero minus 1000 feet."

The woman, regaining her composure, replied, "Sorry Henry. I will need the 23 digit code times 2 for that."

Henry knew what was next. He had memorized these numbers so well that he dreamed of them. Slowly he began pushing the numbers on the face of the phone one by one. He must repeat the entire 23 digit sequence two times without error. This kind of security was necessary. Henry had just ordered the death of over 6,000 men, women and children; including himself.

CHAPTER 8

DAY 5: August 31, 10:23 AM; Pathology conference room ...

Dr. Catlen began, "The reason I called this meeting is to correlate all the data we have on John Doe, Tracy Anderson and the late Dan Nichols. I want to send everything we have back to the people at CDC as soon as possible. Phil, how is Tracy doing today?"

David thought Henry looked like he was under a lot of stress right now. His manner was very business like. He was less a friend lately and more Colonel.

"She's getting stronger by the hour. I will probably send her home tomorrow," Phil reported joyfully. "Frankly, we have never seen anything like it. The young girl is apparently in full remission. Bone marrow samples don't show a trace of cancer. I only wish I could say we had something to do with her recovery, but as you know she was never put on therapy after the incident with Dan."

"And the tissue samples from Dan and Tracy?" Henry continued. "Do you have those results, Lawrence?"

"Yes, and they are all bad. Dan Nichols' tissue samples taken at autopsy show the same kind of intra-nuclear inclusions that the alien's cells do. Also, his whole body seemed to be undergoing some massive cellular change. It was as though every cell was dividing at the time of death."

171

"Some of Tracy's cells," the pathologist continued, "also contain the inclusions, however, as Phil has reported, her malignancy seems to have vanished. And it looks like she may be clearing the viral infection. I wish I could understand why the invasion of Dan's cells by the new virus killed him, while Tracy lives. I don't know, maybe her younger body was just better able to withstand the shock."

"And the alien, Dave, how is he progressing this morning? Is the decalcification and swelling of his skull continuing?"

"Yes it is Henry, and, we still aren't able to understand what is happening. Outside of basic nursing care we aren't doing anything."

"O.K. then," Henry proceeded, "would each of you please have written reports on Dave's desk by tonight. Lawrence, I want slides of the tissue samples, electron micrographs and copies of all the lab slips as well. Can you handle that?"

"Sure, I guess so," the pathologist answered. "Henry, aren't you rushing things a little here. It may be weeks or months before we really have any idea of what we are dealing with in regards to this virus."

"Sorry doctors, we don't have as long as you think. I guess I owe you an explanation, but it must not leave this room! Understand."

All nodded in agreement.

"An alien virus has infected at least two humans. One is dead, the other patient is still an unknown. Tracy could get worse and quickly die. We just don't know. The alien is obviously suffering from more than the trauma of the hit and run accident. He also may not live much longer and there is nothing we can do for him." Henry paused and let what he had been saying sink in, "I was forced to call for sterilization. We cannot risk the life of everyone on the planet."

There was a moment of silence while each of the physicians tried to understand what Henry meant. "You called who for sterilization and what are they going to sterilize?" Dave asked warily.

"I called a special unit that was set up years ago to guard against just this type of danger. Who they are specifically doesn't matter. What they will do does. This entire town must be sterilized; all infectious matter destroyed," Henry answered solemnly.

"How you going to sterilize a town, Henry," chided Phil, "you would have to NUKE the place!"

Henry confirmed the growing fear in the eyes of the men at the conference table, "Exactly."

10:15 PM ...

Bill leaned against the police car staring into the evening sky. He had spent a lot of time out here the last few days still hoping to find something to indicate how the alien had gotten here. Finally he shrugged his shoulders and climbed into the white and black car. After one last look at the terrain he sped off toward the hospital.

For a moment the field behind the receding police car glowed with an eerie yellow-red light and then the darkness returned. Now two dark silhouettes in the pale moonlight stood just off the dirt road. The heads were too large and seven long thin fingers were displayed on each hand.

"I was afraid of this," commented the first alien searching the field for a sign of their tardy companion. "I knew that something had happened when Acemk didn't report back from the survey. I want to go on record as having been against sending such a young surveyor on this kind of mission."

"Yes, yes, Bvkkt. Everyone knows it was I who recommended him for early service. You must admit, however, he had managed one of the highest cerebral activity scores ever measured, and that before neural maturation," Qrrpti defended himself.

"Give me experience over aptitude any time my friend," Bvkkt retorted. "For now however, our job is to find the youngster and get him back to the ship. If he begins metamorphosis on this backward planet he will almost certainly be caught and killed, or die for lack of minimal medical support. Also, I needn't mention his potential for seeding the entire world with HELPER VIRUS before they are ready. Acemk is a walking viral factory right now."

Qrrpti touched a small button on a device attached to his uniform belt. "Let's see if he responds to a homing signal."

Acemk's transom lay beside the sleeping boy's bed. After days of inactivity, several lights on the instruments surface began to blink. A soft beeping emanated from inside the mechanism. Jeffy stirred, but didn't waken.

"No response," Qrrpti reported. "Better try the locator. I presume he is still wearing his support bracelet." The taller alien pushed yet another button on his equipment. "Got him! Bfrratz! My locator makes him out to be in the center of that small town just over there." A long multi-jointed digit pointed the way.

"I haven't heard you use that kind of language in a long time," reprimanded Bvkkt. "No sense wasting any more energy considering what should be. Let's get started. We need to have Acemk back here before morning." The two tall thin figures strode across the field toward town.

Dave slept in the chair at the alien's bedside. He had relieved Hank so the young nurse could see his fiancee tonight. "It was the least he could do," he thought "since the young couple would not live long enough to be married." Dave was too tired to notice the lights on the alien's bracelet flashing brightly in response to Qrrpti's locator signal. Oblivious to his approaching friends, Acemk himself was still comatose.

Outside the room the guard sat in a chair leaning against the wall. His head nodded slowly in concert with the heavy breathing. He was also asleep. The nurses' station was empty when two strange figures strode silently past.

Dave woke as Qrrpti and Bvkkt entered the room. "What! Who are you? How did you get past the guard?" he asked before his eyes cleared of their sleepy veil enough to see the obvious anatomical clues to their identity.

Bvkkt turned to look after his injured friend. Qrrpti reached to his throat and adjusted his translator before speaking. "We have come for our friend," Qrrpti explained simply.

Dave thought about calling the guard, but then something stopped him. He considered the possibilities, then decided quickly. "He was hit by a truck while saving the life of a young boy. We simply didn't know how to help him so we have cared for him as best we could. His condition has worsened because he is infected with a virus that has already killed one of us. He also seems to be suffering from some bone ailment that is destroying his cranial ..." Dave stopped. The two aliens before him looked much like John Doe except for greatly enlarged craniums.

"You don't understand," interrupted Bvkkt. "The HELPER VIRUS isn't a disease, but a designed agent that kills no one. It serves to stabilize the genetic engine of the cell and prevent certain diseases associated with genetic mutation. And, he is undergoing normal cranial enlargement metamorphosis." With these brief explanations the second alien also turned to help the unconscious John Doe.

One of the foreigners assembled a stretcher from thin poles that seemed to strengthen as they were inserted into one another. When assembled they carefully transferred their friend onto the device. After covering him with a thin shinny blanket they began to leave the room.

"Could you help us before you go?" asked Dave taking no action to prevent their departure. One of our patients died after being infected with your HELPER VIRUS. It must act differently in our bodies. You must understand. My people are going to vaporize this entire town tomorrow in an attempt to stop the virus from spreading. Perhaps you could assist us in developing an immunization."

"We're sorry. We cannot stay. We have already risked much by returning to get our comrade, Acemk. The non-intervention covenant is very clear in this area. The only thing I can do is assure you that the virus will disappear from the tissues when it is no longer needed," replied the sympathetic alien.

"Where is his transom?" asked Bvkkt of his companion.

"Do you have his instrument?" Qrrpti asked Dave.

"What instrument? We didn't find anything with him at the accident site," answered Dave.

"Never mind," Bvkkt whispered a little too loud to his companion, "the mechanism will be destroyed during sterilization."

Dave let them leave then sat in the chair at the side of the empty bed and thought about what he had been told.

CHAPTER 9

DAY 6: September 1st, 5:00 AM ...

Dave had been awake all night. He knew he was going to have to explain where John Doe had gone, but he had no regrets concerning allowing his friends to take him. Acemk's only crime had been to try to save a boy's life. Why should he be forced to stay here and be vaporized with the rest of them. The aliens were taking him home - wherever that was - and he would no longer pose a threat to earth.

Bvkkt and Qrrpti had insisted that the virus did not pose a health hazard to humans, but had not explained why Dan Nichols had died. If the virus had not killed him then the medication must have, but toxicology had tested the cytotoxin cocktail and found it to be good. On the other hand Tracy suffered no ill effects from her infection, but rather had gone into remission.

Dave walked slowly out into the hall. The security guard was awake now. "You can go, Arthur," Dave instructed. "We won't be needing a guard anymore."

"Sorry, Dr. Smith." The guard understood his dismissal to mean the patient had died.

Dave sat exhausted at the nurses' station. Absently he followed the lines of a red petal with his finger. "Roses! Who keeps putting these flowers on the ward?"

The duty nurse ran to the desk. "Sorry, Dave, my boyfriend keeps sending me these and I forget to put them in back." The nurse picked up the small vase and began to leave.

"Wait!" Dave jumped from the chair. He moved over to the nurse and, burying his head in the roses, breathed deeply through his nose.

"Dave, are you insane! Your allergies! You will be sneezing and sniffling around here all day," commented the nurse pulling away the bouquet.

Dave breathed deeply through his nose, looking directly at the nurse. "I don't feel any tickle at all! How do I look?" he asked the nurse.

"A little silly," she replied, "but, I don't see any red eyes. Are you testing some new medication?"

"That's it! That's it! A HELPER VIRUS, of course!" Dave ran down the hall flailing his arms and yelling.

"Poor David," the nurse said under her breath while shaking her head, "too much work."

Cytology lab ...

Dave threw open the door to the lab. "Hi there Kathleen! Is it a beautiful day or what?"

Kathleen visibly jumped at her microscope, but didn't need to look up to know who was there. "So Dave, you been taking lessons on breaking and entering from Phil?" she asked with her eyes still glued to the binocular head on the microscope.

"Huh? Listen I need you to do a special stain for me. O.K.?" Dave continued without trying to understand what she meant about Phil.

"Let me guess. You want chromosomal stains and electron microscopy on your cheek cells. Right?" Kathleen looked up from her work.

"Exactly. And I need it ..."

"Stat!" finished the overworked lab tech getting up from her seat.

"Yes, and could you beep me when you have them done?" continued Dave unwrapping a tongue depressor and handing it to Kathleen while pointing to his mouth with the other hand. "This is really, really important Kathleen. I need this information by early tomorrow morning or I won't need it at all. Understand?" Dave was suddenly very serious.

"Yes, I got it. By tomorrow morning. I can do that if I work all day and night."

Dave ignored the sarcasm, "Good girl." Dave left the lab and headed for his office. He had a lot of thinking and reading to do if he was going to save the town from the sterilization scheduled for tomorrow morning. And, oh yes, he guessed he better explain to Henry why John Doe was missing.

Cancer ward ...

Dr. Phil Jones and Henry Catlen met outside Tracy's room. They spoke quietly. "Henry, I want to send Tracy home today. I can't see any reason not to let her spend her last day on the farm with her family."

"Neither can I," agreed Henry. "If you were worried that it would put her out of range of the nuclear device tomorrow, don't be." Then he added sympathetically, "There won't be any suffering, you know. Death for all of us will be instantaneous."

They entered the room together. Tracy was sitting up in bed eating breakfast. She looked wonderful. Her mother and father waited anxiously for Phil to speak. Henry could tell they were concerned about his presence thinking the second doctor might be a sign of bad news.

"Well," began Phil, "all your daughter's tests are normal. There is no sign of malignancy." Mr. Anderson took his wife in his arms; there were tears in both parents' eyes. "You are apparently in full remission, Tracy. Do you know what that means?" Phil had turned his attention to the glowing young patient.

"Yes," she responded enthusiastically, "it means I'm hungry!"

"It also means it's time for you to stop wasting a hospital bed. Why don't you get her dressed, Mrs. Anderson, while your husband and I finish the paperwork to release this girl before she eats this institution into bankruptcy." Phil and Mr. Anderson left the room together. The emotional relief had made the father giddy. As they headed for the elevator he was laughing too loud at jokes that were not too funny.

"Well, I better be going too," Henry said and began to leave the room.

"Phil said you were from Atlanta," Mrs. Anderson stopped the doctor from leaving. "How would you like to come with us to the farm? It's very close and I'll bet you could use a good home cooked meal."

Henry hesitated too long in turning down the invitation. Mrs. Anderson could see he really wanted to get away from the hospital. She insisted, "Really. We would love you to come, wouldn't we Tracy?" The young girl shook her head affirmatively, but continued to eat. It was settled.

CHAPTER 10

DAY 7: September 2nd, 6:50 AM ...

Dave could see the answer to his question in Kathleen's eyes before he asked it. He asked anyway, "So, do you have my stains ready?"

"Yes," she began slowly, "I tried to call Dr. Phlag to show him before I called you, but I can't get hold of him right now."

She handed him a manilla envelope labelled 'Dave Smith, electron micrographs. "I'm sorry, Dave," she stuttered. "Your pictures look just like Dan's did. Maybe there is still something that Dr. Phlag could do ...."

Dave interrupted the concerned technologist. "All right! I knew it! I knew it!" he said joyfully. "Do you have any idea where Dr. Catlen is right now, Kathleen?"

Kathleen couldn't understand what was happening. She had just told Dave his cells were infected in the same way as the late Dan Nichols and the young leukemia patient, Tracy Anderson, and he was happy! "Perhaps one of the effects is dementia," she thought. "No, I haven't seen Dr. Catlen since yesterday. You could see if he left his whereabouts with the hospital operator," she offered.

"Yes, of course," Dave commented and ran from the room yelling, "Thanks kiddo, you don't know how much help you have been!"

The police car sped up to the farmhouse with lights and sirens going full blast. Dave jumped out and ran into the house unannounced. "Henry! Henry! Everything is O.K.! Understand, there is no threat!"

Henry Catlen was sitting at the table having breakfast with the Anderson's. He was not happy at the intrusion. He knew what was going to happen in only a few minutes now, but had almost been able to put it out of his mind. "Stop it, Dave! It is too late!"

"No, no. Listen I'll explain it too you while you make one of your fancy phone calls and stop this thing. Really, I know what I am talking about."

Bill knocked on the kitchen door, "Room for the Sheriff in there?" he called. Mr. Anderson let Bill in.

"Dave, what could you possibly say. Besides I need to place a recall order at the same phone as the original request. There just isn't time ..."

Dave grabbed Henry's arm and pulled him to his feet. "The same phone! Bill, we need to be at the hospital in less than 3 minutes. Can you do that?"

Bill didn't understand what was going on anymore than the Andersons did, but he never turned down a chance to make a high speed run. "I can make it in under 2," he answered already heading for the door.

Dave pushed Henry into the back of the police car, "I'll talk you listen," he commanded. Bill stomped on the throttle and the police car spun and headed for the main road.

"I'm infected too, Henry," Dave began shoving his micrographs at the confused doctor. "The result of this infection is that I don't have allergies anymore. Understand? The aliens were telling the truth. The HELPER VIRUS enters the cells and somehow repairs the genetic damage. That is why Tracy back there is in full remission. The virus has corrected the genetic mutation that caused her leukemia. Now it is disappearing from her tissues."

"That doesn't explain Dan Nichols' sudden death or the death of the cell culture line used to test the alien's specimens," countered Henry still not convinced.

"Yes, yes it does!" Dave was talking faster than Bill was driving at this point, "Dan Nichols was getting well. We killed him. Remember, Lawrence said that it looked like all the cells in his body were dividing when he died. That is how the HELPER VIRUS works. It stimulates division of our cells, but oversees that the genetic information is corrected during division. Right in the middle of Dan's transformation to healthy cells, we gave him a cytotoxin that kills all rapidly dividing cells. Normally that would only kill fast growing cancer cells, but this time it killed almost every cell in his body, good and bad. The virus didn't kill Dan Nichols. I repeat, we did."

"And the cell cultures?" Henry was listening now.

"The cell line wasn't killed. It was cured. Cell cultures depend on malignant cells that will continue to grow in bottles indefinitely. Our cell line was infected with the alien virus and cured of its malignancy just like Tracy. The cells died out because healthy human tissue cells won't grow in bottles! Understand Henry? The virus even cures cell cultures!"

"We must hurry," Henry was talking to Bill now. "I would guess I have less than 4 minutes to place that call."

The police car lunged forward, sliding from side to side down the road. Dave guessed they might die before the bomb could be dropped. "You must not have an accident, Bill! If we crash over 6000 people will die," Dave told his friend. Bill's head jerked around to look into the back seat. "The road, Bill, just look at the road!"

The police car screamed up to the medical center and slid to a stop just before hitting the telephone booth outside the main door. Henry dashed out and ran to the booth. The door was stuck again. Henry pushed and pulled frantically, but couldn't loosen the hinges. The door was locked closed once and for all by the warped hardware. "Shoot the door, Bill!" screamed Dave, "Now Bill, now! Get that door open!"

Bill drew his 45 and held it to the top of the broken door.

"Don't hit the phone line, just the door hinge," warned Henry.

"Blamm! Blamm!" The 45 caliber weapon boomed to life. The phone booth door jerked violently and fell open. Henry jumped inside and picked up the receiver while pieces of glass and metal were still falling around him. Bill and Dave waited breathlessly.

Henry hung up the phone and turned to the other two men, "No problem. They said I had over 30 seconds to spare."

"Who's paying for this telephone booth?" said Bill, "I'm not paying for this thing. You guys told me to shoot off the door. By the way, why did I do all this anyway?"

CHAPTER 11

DAY 55: October 20th, 2:00 PM ...

Jeffy and Tracy walked hand in hand down the dusty road to see Big Red. Although the fall air was cold and crisp, the two youngsters continued to play without coats. As they passed the spot in Baker's field where Jeffy had seen the heroic stranger, they stopped. He remembered the events that had happened here, and the bitterness he had been feeling over Tracy's illness. He looked down at the exotic toy, gripped in his other hand. The small lights never blinked nor did it issue soft beeps anymore, but the boy's imagination was still intact. He raised the instrument quickly and pointed it at his sister's middle. "Pow! Pow! Take that," the playful youngster said.

Tracy fell back and threw her free hand in the air feigning bullet wounds. Her sweatshirt raised momentarily above the waist of her jeans exposing her bear midsection.

Jeffy noticed the angry red-brown scar from a childhood accident was missing. "Hey, Sis, what happened to the big scar on your tummy?" inquired Jeffy.

"I don't know. It went away," she replied pulling her sweatshirt back in place and shrugging her shoulders.

Jeffy looked adoringly at his now healthy sister. "I'm glad you are O.K. now. Do you think God made you well because I asked Him to?"

Tracy squeezed her brother's hand. "Are we going to go see Big Red or not?"

The two children turned and ran, shouting and waving, toward their big friend grazing in the field ahead. Tracy's remission was permanent. A friendly virus protected her from further cancer.

Glossary

accelerate   to increase the speed.

adrenaline   a hormone secreted by adrenal glands located on top of the kidneys. The hormone speeds up the heart beat and in other ways prepares the body to handle emergency situations.

aerodynamic   shaped to allow air to move around an object as easily as possible.

amidships   in the middle of a ship or boat between the bow (front) and stern (back).

anatomical   having to do with the shape and structure of the body.

anemic   a condition in which the blood lacks the proper amount of hemoglobin. Hemoglobin carries oxygen to the body from the lungs and is what makes the red blood cells red in color.

antecubital   in the bend of the arm opposite the elbow.

antithesis   the exact opposite of an idea.

arteries — the thick walled blood vessels that carry blood from the heart to the rest of the body.

artifacts — in microscopy: flaws made during the handling or staining of the material.

asphyxiated — death due to lack of oxygen or excess carbon dioxide in the blood.

autopsy — examination of a body after death.

ballistic — the path of an object that is powered and guided only at the first part of its flight (such as the bullet from a gun).

Berry Aneurysms — weakening of the blood vessels located at the base of the brain due to ballooning and thinning of the vessel's walls.

binocular — having two eyepieces so that both eyes may be used at the same time.

biological units — living things

biological hazard hood — a special cabinet closed on all sides except for a small opening in front for a person's arms. Air flow across the opening is controlled to prevent the passage of germs.

cancer   a group of uncontrolled, fast growing cells that push aside healthy tissue and rob the body of nutrients.

cardiopul-monary   having to do with the heart and lung system.

CAT scan   a special machine that takes a large number of x-rays of a patient which a computer assembles into a three dimentional image. Short for **C**omputer **A**ssisted **T**omography.

cell culture   a method of growing human or animal cells in bottles in the laboratory.

ceramic   materials made by cooking nonmetallic minerals, such as clay, at very high temperatures.

cerebral   relating to the brain or intellect.

chemistry   the branch of science dealing with the composition of materials and how they react with one another.

chemotherapy   chemicals placed into the blood to help fight disease.

chromosomal patterns   the specific numbers and shapes of chromosomes in a cell. Each species has a characteristic pattern.

chromosome a strand-like body in the nucleus of the cell that carries the genes of heredity.

chronological arranged in order by time.

circuit a path for electric current in an electronic device.

circumference the distance around an object.

Class III hood a biological hood designed for handling very dangerous germs.

comatose a state of very deep sleep from which a patient cannot be awakened.

composite matrix a substance made up of two or more dissimilar materials which shows new and unique properties.

concentric circles of different sizes with the same center.

cornea the layer of clear cells covering the pupil of the eye.

coronary a dangerous medical condition where the heart muscle is damaged because it fails to receive enough blood.

CPU the brain of a computer. Short for **C**entral **P**rocessing **U**nit.

cranial   belonging to the skull.

crash cart   the common name for a hospital cart that has the medicines and equipment needed to treat a patient whose heart and breathing have stopped.

critical mass   sufficient material to cause a reaction. In physics: the amount of radioactive material required to begin an atomic explosion.

cytology   the branch of science that deals with the structure and function of cells.

cytotoxin   a chemical used to treat certain kinds of cancer. The chemical usually works by killing all fast growing cells.

decalcification   loss of the calcium that strengthens bones and teeth.

decibel   a measure of sound or noise level.

dementia   loss of normal intelligence that may occur with disease or age.

dichroic   the property of some materials to reflect light of some colors and let other colors pass through.

digits   fingers.

DNA — an inherited string of genes found in the cell nucleas which specifies the individual traits of that organism. Short for **D**eoxyribo**n**ucleic **A**cid.

dot matrix printhead — printer head that uses a row of 9 or more tiny metal pins to strike an inked ribbon and thus draw letters with a pattern of small dots.

drag coefficient — the forces of air molecules that slow the motion of an object such as an airplane.

ecological niche — a part of the world where a particular animal finds it easiest to get food and protect itself.

electrolytes — salts such as sodium chloride that are dissolved in the body's fluids.

electromagnetic spectrum — the entire range of radiated energy including radio waves, infrared, visible light, ultraviolet, x-rays, and gamma waves.

electron microscopy — magnifying an object with a microscope that focuses a beam of electrons rather than visible light waves. Capable of magnifications thousands of times greater than the conventional light microscope.

engineering   the science of using the properties of matter and natural energy sources to make buildings, machines, and products for man's use.

epidemic   an outbreak of disease that affects a large number of the people living in an area.

extra-terrestrial   a living being not born on earth.

extra chromosomal DNA   strands of genes that are not part of the chromosomes found in the cell nucleus.

fixation   a method of preserving tissue specimens.

flora   the harmless germs found on the skin and in the gut of all animals.

formic acid   a colorless, but strong smelling organic acid that is found in most ants and some other insects.

frequency   the number of vibrations, waves, cycles, or other events per second. The greater the frequency of a sound, the higher the pitch.

friction   force resisting the motion of an object.

g forces the force on any object relative to the earth's gravity. A 100 pound object weighs 200 pounds under a two g force and 300 pounds under a 3 g force etc.

galaxy a large cluster of stars. Our Sun is part of The Milky Way galaxy.

genetic having to do with genes whcih are short segments of DNA that specify an inherited trait.

genetic mutation an accidental change in the structure of a gene.

graphite the soft mineral used for pencil lead. A form of carbon.

gravitational field the force that tends to draw two or more bodies, such as the Moon and Earth, together.

gurney a small bed with wheels used to move patients around a hospital.

gyroscope (gyro) a wheel or disc spinning rapidly about one axis which tends to resist any force to change the angle of the axis of rotation.

hardware the electronic circuits that make up a computer.

harmonic resonance the natural vibration of any object that occurs when it absorbs energy from another.

helium a light weight, chemically inert gas commonly used to fill balloons.

hematocrit the percentage of a person's blood that consists of the red blood cells (normally 35% to 45%).

hexagonal having 6 sides.

hologram a three dimensional picture or image.

hydrofoils underwater plates or skis attached by struts to a boat for lifting the hull out of the water as speed increases.

hydrogen a colorless, odorless and explosive gas. The lightest element.

immortal never dying.

immunization also called vaccination. Injection of an altered or killed germ into a healthy person to stimulate the body to produce antibodies and thus protect the person from that disease.

inclusion body
rounded or oval structure inside a cell that is characteristic of certain viral diseases.

induced electric current
electric current in a metal object created as a result of a changing magnetic field.

inflammation
a localized body response to cellular injury characterized by redness, swelling, heat, and pain.

intelligence
the ability to understand.

intergalactic
between galaxies.

intra-nuclear inclusions
an unusual structure found inside the cell nucleus that is characteristic of certain viral diseases such as the simple cold sore.

intravenous (I.V.)
delivered through a hollow needle or tube directly into a patients vein.

ion
electrically charged particle.

ionization
the process of producing electrically charged particles.

knots
nautical miles per hour. One knot = a distance of 1/60 th of a degree at the Earth's equator , or 6,080.2 feet.

Glossary

laparotomy   surgical section or incision of the abdominal wall exposing the intestines for repair or diagnosis.

larynx   the voice box that holds the vocal cords.

LASER   a device which synchronizes the normal vibrations of light to produce an extremely compact beam. Short for **L**ight **A**mplification by **S**timulated **E**mission of **R**adiation.

LED   A small light-producing semiconductor which commonly glows red and is used in various calculator and stereo displays. Short for **L**ight **E**mitting **D**iode.

leukemia   a cancer of the blood-forming organs that usually results in an improper number of white cells in the blood.

Mach   the speed of sound at sea level (about 1087 feet per second or 741 miles per hour).

magnetically   as a result of a magnetic force.

malignant   a cancer. Uncontrolled cell growth that spreads to other parts of the body.

mass   the quantity of matter in an object.

metamorphosis   a series of changes in a living organism that result in its transforming to another physical form. Common among insects.

meteor   Shooting stars. Solid matter, such as a rock, that burns brightly in the atmosphere as it falls to Earth from space.

methodologies   a number of procedures or rules used by a particular science.

microbial   referring to germs such as bacteria, yeast or viuses.

microcosm   a little world within a bigger universe.

microscopically thin   so thin as to need a microscope to see its thickness.

microscope   an instrument that uses multiple glass lenses to magnifiy tiny particles or germs so they are visible to the eye.

microscopy   using a microscope.

microtome   an instrument for cutting very thin sections of tissue so they can be looked at under a microscope.

milligram   1/1000 th of a gram. 28,571 milligrams = 1 ounce.

monolith   something of tremendous size and strength.

morgue   a place where the bodies of people are temporarily kept until burial.

nanoseconds   1 billionth (1 / 1,000,000,000) of a second.

neural   having to do with nerves.

Nobel laureate   someone who has won the Nobel Prize. The Nobel Prize is a great honor given only for major discoveries or advances in a given field of study.

nova   an exploding star.

ominous   threatening, dangerous, risky.

ophthalmologist   a medical doctor who specializes in diseases and defects of the eye.

ophthalmoscope   an instrument used to look through the pupil of the eye to see the retina at the back of the eye.

orb   a ball, globe or sphere.

orbit   the path an object takes when it moves in a circular manner about another body, usually under the force of gravity.

	The Earth's orbit takes it around the Sun once each year.
organism	a living thing.
orthopedic	pertaining to the correction or prevention of deformities, especially of the skeleton.
oscillating	vibrating.
peripheral vision	ability to see things off to the left or right side of the direct line of sight.
phenomenon	an observable event.
phosphorus	a non-metallic chemical element that in pure form burns spontaneously in air. A component of teeth and bone.
photoelectric	having to do with the generation of an electric current directly from light.
photoelectric cell	device with a light-sensitive material that generates an electric current when exposed to a light source.
physiology	the study of the functions and activities of organs, tissues, and cells.
Planetary Society	Established in 1980, this society is dedicated to the exploration of space by man

and the search for other intelligence in the universe. Publishers of *The Planetary Report.*

planetoid asteroid-sized objects in space.

plasma stream in physics, a jet of ionized gas.

precluded prevented, hindered, stopped.

propulsion the action of driving forward or ahead (e.g. jet propulsion).

prosthesis an artificial device to replace a missing part of the body.

protoplasm the more or less fluid organic substances and water that make up the nucleus and cytoplasm of cells.

prototype the original model.

proximity closeness, nearness, vicinity.

quiescent inactive.

radar device used to locate objects by means of high frequency radio waves.

ramjet a jet engine that has an opening in front to collect air which is compressed in the combustion chamber and mixed with fuel.

remission   a temporary decrease in the symptoms of a disease.

resin   a member of a large class of plastic-like synthetic products that may be unusually strong yet flexible.

retina   the back of the eye that is coated with special cells that are sensitive to light.

RNA   strands of genetic material that read the DNA and make the proteins to express particular traits. If the DNA *says* curly hair, RNA builds hair proteins with lots of sulfide bonds so it tends to curl. Short for **Ribonucleic Acid**.

saline   a salt solution.

satellite   a small body orbiting a larger planet or sun.

semicircular canals   the loop-shaped tubular parts of the inner ear that make up a sensory organ used to maintain balance.

software   the program directing a computer's functions (see hardware).

Glossary

solar system   the sun together with all the planets and asteroids that orbit around it.

solenoids   an electrically powered magnetic switch.

sonic blast   a very strong burst of sound.

spectrographic patterns   the specific pattern of intensities of various colors of light from an object.

spectrum   with visible light: the ordered separation of the colors from blue through red as in a rainbow.

stat   in medicine: to be done immediately.

static electricity   electrical charge built up on an object.

stratosphere   that portion of the atmosphere more than 7 miles above the earth.

sublimating   passing directly from solid to a gas or gas to solid without going through a liquid stage.

subliminal   acting without conscious awareness.

subset   a collection of data that is itself part of a larger assortment (eg: odd numbers are a subset of all numbers).

superconduct-ing magnet
an electromagnet made of material which is a superconductor.

super-conductor
a material that offers absolutely no resistance to electrical current at low temperatures.

synchronous emission
energy or mass ejected all with the same period of vibration.

synchronize
to cause to happen at the same time.

synergistically
each increasing the effectiveness of the other (eg: some medicines are more effective when given together than if given separately).

technologies
groups of related methods for performing specific jobs.

telemetry
the measuring of quantities such as speed or temperature and transmitting the results to a distant station.

teleportation
to move an object without physical contact.

template
a pattern or guide.

theoretical
having to do with an educated belief or hypothesis based on previous experience, but without direct proof.

Glossary

titanium   a light-weight, strong metallic element.

toxicology   a science that deals with poisons and their effect on living organisms.

trajectory   the curved path that a moving body describes in flight.

transformer   device that converts electric current in one coil of wire to a different voltage and current in the second coil.

translucent   a material which transmits and diffuses light so that objects beyond cannot be clearly distinguished (eg: frosted glass).

transom   an optical device for measuring angles and distances between two points.

umbilici   plural of umbilicus: a depression in the middle of the abdomen where the umbilical cord was attached (the navel).

universe   the entire celestial cosmos including all stars and planets in existence.

vacuum   empty space without atmosphere.

variable   a quantity that is subject to change.

velocity   speed and direction.

venous   having to do with the relatively thin walled vessels (veins) that return blood from all parts of the body to the heart.

videophone   a telephone that transmits both the voice and a video picture.

weightlessness   the condition of having no weight which occurs when there are no forces acting on a body (eg: no gravity).

x-rays   electromagnetic radiation having the characteristics of light, but a wavelength about 50 times shorter than visible light.

TadAleX would appreciate your returning this response card after reading **Molecular Ramjet and other bedtime stories.** All comments will be read by the author and publishers.

Was the purchase price ($_____) of the book? high / ok / low . Where purchased _____

Which story was your favorite?   **Molecular Ramjet** / **The Game** / **Stranger in Town**

Please comment

_____

Your age: <10   10-15   16-20   21-30   30-40   >40.   Did you find the glossary useful?   yes   no

If you purchased this book for a child list: age(s) ⦧ ⦧ ⦧
                                                sex(m/f) ⦧ ⦧ ⦧
                                                grade level ⦧ ⦧ ⦧

Did you read this book to or with your child? yes no .

Your estimate of the grade level necessary to enjoy these stories. _____

Name:_____

Address:_____

City:_____ State:_____

Zip:_____

Please print clearly

**TadAleX
MRJ Reader Response
P.O. BOX NUMBER 78582
Seattle, Washington 98178**